From the Files of

Madison Finn

Read all the books about *Madison Finn*!

Coming Soon!

Don't miss the Super Edition

To Have and to Hold

From the Files of
Madison Finn

Off the Wall

By Laura Dower

VOLO

HYPERION
New York

Printed in the United States of America

First Edition
1 3 5 7 9 10 8 6 4 2

The main body of text of this book is set in 13-point Frutiger Roman.

ISBN 0-7868-1737-2

Visit www.madisonfinn.com

For *my* honey bear, Myles

The cursor on Madison's classroom computer blinked slowly, and Madison kicked her foot against the bottom of her chair. Sometimes school computers could be really annoying. Her laptop from home worked much faster, with its alternating starburst and rolling arrow cursors.

Unfortunately, Mrs. Wing didn't allow personal laptops in computer lab. So, even though Madison liked to bring her laptop to school, she didn't bring it into that class. Madison couldn't very well argue with her favorite teacher in the whole school.

The computer room filled up quickly. Everyone made a beeline for the usual seats. Walter "Egg" Diaz and Drew Maxwell, two of Madison's closest guy friends, shuffled in and sat down at computer terminals on either side of Madison. The three always sat near one another in computer lab—mostly so they could gossip and exchange goofy glances in the middle of class.

Today Egg and Drew chatted about Splat, a new video game from their joint collection. The game was part paint ball and part action-adventure, but it sounded dumb to Madison. She'd much rather have spent time writing or chatting online than hurling virtual paint balls at imaginary bull's-eyes. Bored, she turned away from their conversation, moving her chair to face the desk behind her. She was shocked to discover Lance, another kid in class, power-picking his nose.

Ewww. Gross.

Madison's stomach heaved. Sometimes guys in her class could be so disgusting. And the whole experience was made worse by the fact that Madison had sneaking suspicions that maybe Lance liked her—in *that* way. Lately, he always seemed to show up when she was waiting at the lockers. And he would always wind up in a seat close to hers.

"Howdy," Lance chirped. He obviously didn't know he'd been caught picking.

"Howdy," Madison said, not looking directly at him. He had a piece of toast stuck in his teeth, too. That was what he should have been picking, Madison thought. *Poor Lance.*

The truth was that Madison didn't like Lance in

that way, because he didn't make her heart go *pa-ping*. Not like Hart Jones, the crush she'd had all year long. Hart was her dreamiest of dream guys. He could pick his nose and Madison wouldn't even mind.

The bell to announce the start of class went off, and everyone settled into his or her seat. But after two minutes, Mrs. Wing still hadn't arrived.

"I wonder where she is," Madison said.

"She's never late, is she?" Egg replied.

"Maybe she got stuck in traffic," Lance said.

"Traffic? What—like in the hallway?" Drew said, raising his eyebrows.

Madison giggled. "Come on, you, Mrs. Wing's probably talking to someone, and she's lost track of time."

But Madison wondered if that really could be true. She gazed up at the clock. A full five minutes had passed. Mrs. Wing *was* never late.

"Holy cow!" a voice boomed.

Madison jumped as a tall, thin guy wearing thick, red-rimmed glasses bounded into the classroom. "It took me a century to find you cats," he said.

"You *cats*?" Egg whispered, rolling his eyes.

Drew snorted.

Madison felt like giggling, but she was too confused. Who was this strange man—and what had he done with Mrs. Wing?

"I'm Freddy Franks," the guy said, introducing himself. He went around the room asking everyone else to volunteer their names. Mr. Franks said he had a picture-perfect, photographic memory. He proved it by reciting back to the class the full name of everyone seated inside the computer lab.

Egg and Drew looked super-impressed. But Madison wasn't. She didn't have time for mind tricks. Not when Mrs. Wing was missing. Wasn't anyone else the least bit curious about her whereabouts?

Madison raised her hand high into the air.

"Um . . . yes, Miss Madison Finn," Mr. Franks said, getting her name right on the first try.

"Where is our teacher?" Madison asked. "I mean, is she out sick?"

Mr. Franks lifted his hands. "Haven't a clue," he said. "I just know she's out today and probably for the rest of next week."

"Is she on vacation?" Madison asked.

"As I said, I just don't know," Mr. Franks said. "Sorry."

Madison imagined Mrs. Wing sitting at home, sicker than sick, sneezing and coughing and unable even to move a computer mouse. Something bad must have happened for Mrs. Wing to desert her class like this. Madison's imagination took a flying leap.

She pictured Mrs. Wing alone in a dark trench coat, on a crowded plane, wearing big sunglasses, running from something. . . .

She envisioned Mrs. Wing captured by strange little aliens who came in through the computer. . . .

"Ohhhhh, *Mad*-i-son!" Mr. Franks's singsong voice interrupted Madison's daydream. She looked around and saw her classmates staring back at her.

Egg and Drew cracked up. The rest of the class followed. Soon everyone was laughing heartily—at Madison's expense. She turned purple, like Charlie Brown in a Peanuts cartoon.

"Madison, could you help walk the class through the school Web site?" Mr. Franks asked. "I have notes from your teacher, Mrs. Wing. She says *you're* the expert around here."

Madison felt her cheeks, hot and still blushing.

Steadily, she braced herself and opened the Far Hills Junior High home page on her computer screen. As her classmates and their substitute teacher gathered around Madison's monitor, she slowly explained how she updated the Web site. The class worked together to download photos from the recent bake and book sale. They also posted midseason sports team schedules on the site.

By the time the end-of-class bell rang, Madison's blush had finally faded, and the rest of the class seemed to have forgotten her mega-embarrassment.

Of course, she hadn't.

Madison wanted out of that room right away! She headed straight for the door, bypassing Egg, Drew, and Lance on her way.

"Wait! Hey! Aren't you going to lunch, Maddie?" Drew yelled out after her.

"Yeah," Egg teased. "You're an expert at that, too."

Madison sighed. *Couldn't the boys just let her make a clean getaway?*

She playfully put up her fists. "Wanna take this outside?" she joked.

"Get out of here," Egg cracked. "I would whomp you."

Madison giggled. Egg would tease her forever. It was useless to fight it. So she and the boys headed for the lunchroom together. As per the usual routine, their group would meet up with other friends at the big orange table at the back of the cafeteria.

Once inside the lunchroom, Madison grabbed a hot, just-washed tray and tossed a banana and a carton of chocolate milk onto it. Gilda Z, the lunch lady, served her an overflowing cup of "Amazing Orzo Soup." It didn't look so amazing, though. It had little red and green things floating on top.

"Hey, Maddie!" Aimee Gillespie cried from the front of the lunch line. She hustled toward Madison with an apple in one hand and a pear in the other. Aimee, dancer extraordinaire and Madison's BFF, always ate fruit or granola or something equally healthful for her lunch.

Walking behind Aimee was Fiona Waters, Madison's other BFF in seventh grade. Fiona, unlike Aimee, *rarely* ate health food. Her lunch tray was piled high with lasagna, vegetables, two packages

6

of pretzels, a slice of chocolate cake, a yogurt cup, and a bottle of water.

"Hey, Maddie," Fiona said.

"You won't believe what happened in computer lab!" Madison cried. "Mrs. Wing blew off class. She never showed up."

"Whoa," Fiona said. "So you got a free period?"

Aimee made a face. "That's impossible. We never get to miss class around here. I bet you had some dorky substitute. Right, Maddie?"

"We did! And the sub said Mrs. Wing would be gone *all next week*. Something is wrong, I know it," Madison said.

"HEY, SIS!" Chet Waters pounced on Fiona and shoulder-checked her, nearly knocking the food off her tray.

"Hey, yourself!" Fiona growled. "Now, back off, before I dump this on your head."

Madison and Aimee loved watching battles between the Waters twins. Fiona and Chet were always arguing about something.

Egg, Drew, and Hart stood in line after Chet, grumbling about the hot-lunch selection. Within minutes, the group had all gotten their food and were seated together at the back of the room, picking at their lunches and whispering about other classmates. Madison was convinced that boys liked to gossip even more than girls did. Egg certainly liked to.

7

"Hey, Maddie," Drew cried. "Did you hear about the new page on bigfishbowl.com?"

Bigfishbowl.com was the most popular Web site with Madison and her friends. It had chat rooms, a fortune-telling blowfish, and all sorts of cool surveys.

Madison nodded. The site had recently added a new section called Trend Talk, where kids could post messages to each other.

"That's nothing!" Egg said. "I know a way cooler site, called The Wall. My sister told me about it."

According to Egg, The Wall was a giant bulletin board where kids could post ideas, comments, and gossip of all kinds. Madison thought she knew about most of the new Web sites, but she hadn't heard anything about The Wall.

"The Wall is way better than bigfishbowl.com," Egg said. "That has too many moderators. It's so babyish. The Wall has cooler bulletin boards. You really should check it out."

"Hmmm," Madison said, intrigued.

"Don't do it!" Someone shrieked across the lunchroom. Madison glanced over and saw Ivy Daly seated a few tables away. Poison Ivy had been Madison's mortal enemy for the past few years. She was laughing out loud—really loud—with her drones "Phony" Joanie and Rose "Thorn." No matter where she was in school, Madison always seemed to cross paths with Ivy. Today was no exception.

Ivy caught Madison staring. She mouthed the words, "What's *your* problem?"

Madison looked back down at her food. Ivy had the unique ability to leave Madison speechless.

Meanwhile, Madison's friends continued to blab about The Wall, soccer, chocolate cake, flying monkeys, and anything else that happened to pop into their heads.

After school, Aimee and Fiona headed toward their after-school activities, while Madison headed home. She had a plan: to check out The Wall. So, as soon as she arrived, Madison said her hellos to Phin, her adorable pug, clicked on her laptop, and went online.

Egg had given Madison the link to get onto The Wall, so she typed it in. The home page came up right away. Madison saw a flashing purple banner that read:

WELCOME TO THE WALL!
POST YOUR DEEP THOUGHTS NOW!

Then, in smaller print (almost unreadable as far as Madison was concerned, since she had to lean so close to the screen to make out the words), were the comments:

For your safety and to keep the bulletin board fun, please DO NOT: swear, flood the

message board, give out personal info,
exchange photos, post other people's
addresses, or use false screen addresses.
Above all, do not be disrespectful to
others on The Wall. These boards are
reserved for 9- to 14-year-olds only.

Madison scanned the rules and clicked a flashing blue square that said "Let's Go!" The monitor went dark for a second. Then it started to glow around the edges.

READY TO BREAK IT DOWN?

A sound like shattered glass blared out of Madison's computer speakers, and even Phinnie jumped. Madison lowered the volume and watched as a multicolored, brick "wall" on the screen broke apart to reveal a long list of bulletin-board topics.

```
THE WALL
HOT TOPICS
School
Sports
Current Events
Beauty
Games
Parents
Gossip
```

Madison immediately clicked on GOSSIP. It was the one Egg had recommended. Another long list of postings came up on the screen, which showed a general posting, "Name," and the number of responses it had received.

```
HOT TOPICS: GOSSIP
What should I do???       3
Angry grrrl              25
Pet peeve                13
Friends-n-enemies         8
Yoo-hoo                  17
Believe THIS              9
Help help help           10
Is this place confusin   15
pretty in pink            5
jokes on u               22
```

Madison was about to click on one of the subtopics when Mom walked into her room, arms crossed over her chest.

"Are you doing your homework?" Mom asked.

Madison hit a key that made the screen go blue. Her new zebra-and-wildebeest screen saver flashed on. Madison always had wild and endangered animals on her screen savers.

"You look guilty," Mom said, tapping her foot. "Where are your books? Didn't we have a conversation about Internet use being allowed only *after* the homework is finished?"

"Yeah," Madison said. She bent over and grabbed Phinnie, pulling the dog into her lap. She stroked his ears so she wouldn't have to look up.

"Dinner will be ready in about half an hour. And I want you to get some homework done before then," Mom said sternly. "None of this staying up late to work on book reports, okay?"

Madison nodded.

As soon as Mom had left the room, however, Madison immediately clicked back on to The Wall. The Gossip screen came into view. Then an Insta-Message appeared in the corner of the screen.

Aimee was online.

```
<BalletGrl>: Whassup chica?
<MadFinn>: I'm ok. WAY?
<BalletGrl>: Huge newz so
    Ihadtowrite right away
<MadFinn>: 8>O
<BalletGrl>: Mom & Dad said yes to
    making puppies for Blossom,
    finally
<MadFinn>: GOOH!!!!!
<BalletGrl>: Isn't this the coolest
    EVER???
```

Ever since Aimee and Madison had gotten their family dogs a few years earlier, they'd talked about how much fun it would be to breed them together. Madison always thought that Blossom, Aimee's basset hound, would be the best match for her pug, Phineas T. Finn.

```
<MadFinn>: When?
<BalletGrl>: Sometime next week
    maybe. Dad made an appt.
<MadFinn>: an appt?
<BalletGrl>: an appt like an
    appointment at the breeder, they
    have a male basset hound that is
    looking 4 a m8. It's like
    looooove connection for dogs.
```

Madison stopped typing. She stared at the screen.

```
<BalletGrl>: Maddie r u there???
```

Breeder? Love connection? Another basset hound? What was Aimee talking about?

Phin wriggled around by Madison's feet, trying to get comfortable on the rug. Madison patted the top of his head and whispered in his ear.

"Oh, Phinnie, I'm so sorry," Madison said, as if Phin knew that he'd just been cut from the father-to-be list.

```
<BalletGrl>: HELLLLOOOOOO???? CML?
```

Madison didn't know what to write to Aimee. So

instead of typing a quick response like *I gotta run* or *C u l8r*, Madison abruptly ended her Insta-Message and headed back to The Wall.

It was way better to read someone else's gossip than to worry about her own feelings—at least for right now.

Chapter 2

Phin kicked Madison in his sleep. Hard.

He'd curled up near the top of Madison's pillows, and his little paws were jerking as if he had been dreaming he was running a race.

Madison's mind raced, too, as she lay there in the half-dark, waiting for her alarm clock to buzz. She had set it to wake up on the early side, even though it was Saturday. Madison had thought a night's sleep would make all her icky feelings about Aimee and the puppies-to-be go away.

But it hadn't.

The sun shone in through Madison's bedroom window, but it was still cold in her room, so she snuggled further under the covers.

Beep. Beep. Beep.

She punched off the alarm button and stared up at her ceiling. She saw things she'd never noticed before. Peeling paint, a dusty cobweb in the corner . . .

Dingdong.

A groggy Madison fell out of bed and pressed her nose up to the window. Was there a delivery truck parked in the driveway? Had Dad come over to visit early today? She saw only Mom's car parked there. Who could be ringing the—?

"Rowf rowf!"

Madison heard a bark. She caught her breath. It was Aimee at the door—she knew it. That was Blossom's bark.

Phin knew, too. The moment he recognized his doggy friend's hello, Phinnie began to prance around the room.

"Maddie!" Mom's voice called out from the upstairs hallway. "Are you dressed? I just got out of the shower. Can you get the door, please?"

"Oh, Mom." Madison groaned. "Do I have to? I'm still in bed." Her heart thumped. She couldn't face Aimee. Not after what had happened the night before.

Mom came to the doorway of Madison's room in a bathrobe and slippers, a wet towel wrapped around her head.

"Honestly, Maddie, I don't know what's gotten

into you these days. I'm dripping wet. I need you to get the door."

"Mom, please. PLEASE," Madison pleaded. "I think it's Aimee."

"So? All the more reason for you just to answer it. She's your best friend, Maddie. . . ."

"Mom, you don't understand. We had a fight. A big fight."

"What? When?" Mom looked concerned. "You didn't tell me anything about—"

Dingdong.

"Madison Finn." Mom crinkled up her nose. "What's going on?"

"I just can't talk to Aimee now," Madison said. "Mom, please do this one thing for me. I'll explain later. Please?"

Mom let out a huge sigh.

"Fine! But afterward, you're telling me *everything*," Mom said. She whirled around, towel and bathrobe on, and headed downstairs.

Madison crawled toward her bedroom entrance so she could eavesdrop. Phin sniffed around the door.

"Aimee! What a surprise!" Madison heard Mom say as she opened the front door.

"Hi, Mrs. Finn," Aimee said. "I came to see Maddie. I thought maybe we could walk the dogs together. . . ."

Madison bit her lip. What would Mom say next?

"Walk the dogs? Oh, I'm sorry, Aim," Mom

answered. "Madison isn't feeling well right now. Can she . . . can she call you later?"

Madison clutched at her pj's and listened close. What would Aimee say next?

"Oh, wow, sick?" Aimee said. She sounded disappointed. "But I just talked to her last night. . . . She seemed fine."

"Yes, but . . ." Mom stalled.

"Well . . . um . . . tell her to call me as soon as she feels better, okay? Fiona and I are hanging out later. We might go ice skating. And if Maddie wants to come, that would be cool."

"Okay, dear," Mom said sweetly. "I'll tell her."

That was all Madison needed to hear. She scooted back over to her bed and bounced down onto the edge. "What a close one, Phinnie!" she said. "But Mom saved the day."

"Rowrrrooooo!" Phin howled.

A few moments later, Mom reappeared at Madison's bedroom door, arms folded tightly. She had a Grinch-like scowl on her face.

"Start talking, young lady," Mom said.
And Madison did.

From: MadFinn
To: Bigwheels
Subject: When Things Fall Apart
Date: Sat 4 Nov 11:47 AM

Bad things come in threes. It's cold. My teacher is MIA. My best friend has betrayed me.

Okay, I'm being a little dramatic, I know. But how am I supposed to feel when my BFF in the whole planet goes back on a promise we've had forever and ever?

Aimee and I said a long time ago that our puppies would make puppies one day. It was like a dream of mine. And now that she's ready with her dog, it turns out that my dog isn't the lucky dad. I know we didn't make a formal pact or anything, but isn't a friend's word supposed to count for something?

Okay. I shouldn't whine, because there are poor, starving people in the world, but I feel soooo crummy and it's hard to think about anything but this. Does that make me a bad person? Am I obsessing over nothing?

I wish it would snow or something. I hate winter when nothing happens except lots of cold and more cold and blah, blah, blah.

Help me!

Yours till the head aches,

Maddie

xoxox

P.S. My friend Egg told me about
this new bulletin board site, The
Wall. It's cool. Have u seen it?

Madison hit SEND.

After Mom's strategic save with Aimee, Madison
had been feeling a little better. But it was communication with her keypal Bigwheels, aka Victoria, that
made Madison feel best of all. Bigwheels always
knew the right things to say to ease Madison's
anxiousness about friends, school, and parent stuff.
Hopefully, she'd respond right away to Madison's
e-mail.

After logging off, Madison headed back into the
kitchen to grab her jacket. Mom suggested that
Madison plan something for Saturday afternoon, to
raise her spirits, rather than just moping around the
house, avoiding friends like Aimee. A good place to
visit was the animal clinic, of course. What better
place for Madison to go when she was bummed out
about puppies . . . than a place where she could visit
lots of puppies? Mom even agreed to drive her there.

20

Best of all, while she was at the clinic, Madison could talk to her friend Dan Ginsburg, the one guy who could *always* make Madison laugh out loud. Dan volunteered at the clinic every Saturday and most weekday afternoons. His mom, Eileen Ginsburg, was the primary veterinary nurse there.

"Have fun with the animals, honey bear," Mom said as she dropped Madison off in front of the clinic. "Phin and I will just be hanging out at home. Call, and we'll come back to pick you up."

Mom gave Madison a big kiss good-bye, and Phin gave Madison an even bigger doggy smooch through the rear window.

The entrance to the clinic was decorated with wreaths and brightly colored lights. Eileen sat behind the front desk of the clinic, helping visitors and their pets. On one side of the room, a woman cradled her French bulldog, and a man held on to his black cat in a box. On the other side of the room, an older woman yipped back at her nippy little terrier, and a couple played with a small, gray ferret on a small, gray leash.

"Hey, Maddie! Dan's in the back!" Eileen yelled. "Go on in." Eileen wore a crazy T-shirt from her T-shirt collection. It said PAWS FOR PEACE and had different muddy animal paw prints all over the front and back.

Madison wandered toward the kennels in the

back. The clinic kept two main groups of animals there: those recovering from medical procedures and those needing to be adopted.

Puppies barked and kittens meowed as Dan cleaned cages. The whole room smelled like wet fur and lemon soap. Madison felt right at home.

"Maddie! I'm so glad you're here. I could use your help big-time," Dan said, tossing Madison a cleaning rag.

"I'm glad you're here, too," Madison told Dan. "It's been a bad day. I need cheering up."

"Try cleaning up dog poop and cat poop," Dan cracked. "That'll cheer you up real fast."

"Ewwwww," Madison groaned. She turned to look inside the cages. "Who's new?"

Dan pointed to a large German shepherd that sat pensive, eyes watering a little. "We're calling him Mr. Serious," Dan said. "Doesn't he look bummed out?"

"Maybe Mr. Serious and I should bond," Madison said. She reached over to his cage and handed him a dog bone cookie from the bin on the floor. Mr. Serious barked and attempted to pace inside his small cage. He grabbed the cookie and licked his chops.

"Hey, he likes you!" Dan cried. "I think he just smiled!"

"You sound surprised," Madison said. "Who doesn't like me?"

"That's my line," Dan cracked.

They both laughed.

"Why are there three cats in here?" Madison asked, pointing to another cage. She read the names on the little card attached to the pen: Winky, Blinky, and Nod. The kittens were orange with white stripes.

"Someone left a litter on this old lady's step," Dan explained. "So she brought 'em here. She kept three, gave up three. Mom and I were thinking of keeping one."

"I wish my mom weren't allergic to cats," Madison said. "She doesn't mind Phinnie for some reason, even though he sheds a lot. . . ."

"Why don't you get one of those hairless cats?" Dan said.

Madison raised an eyebrow. "You mean those naked-looking cats?"

Dan giggled. "Naked?" he repeated.

Madison looked away, a little embarrassed. She tried to change the subject. "Um, Dan, I was wondering," she said, grabbing a fistful of newspapers to line some empty cages. "Has Egg or Drew or any of the guys ever broken a promise they made to you?"

"What kind of promise?" Dan asked. "Egg once said he'd meet me at the lake and he never showed up. Does that count?"

"I guess," Madison said.

"Why are you asking? Did someone break a promise to you?" Dan asked.

Madison nodded. "Yeah. Aimee did—sort of. A couple of years ago when we got our dogs, Blossom and Phin, Aimee said that one day they'd have puppies together. But now, that isn't going to happen."

"So, what's the big deal?" Dan asked.

"A promise is a promise," Madison said. "I've *never* broken one."

"Never?" Dan said. "Look, maybe she just forgot."

Madison looked into a cage and stared down a shih tzu. "What do you think, Pearl?" she asked the pooch. "Do you think it's fair or not?"

"Chill out, Maddie," Dan said. "Phin can have puppies with some other dog. Hey, you have ten to choose from right here," he said, pointing like a game-show host to the cages.

Madison laughed. "Very funny. By the way, where is Dr. Wing today? I haven't seen him once back here. Isn't this usually his busy time?"

Dan scratched his head. "He left yesterday and said he wasn't coming back for a few days. Mom's holding down the fort."

"Where did Dr. Wing go?" Madison asked.

"Who knows?" Dan said.

"You know, Mrs. Wing was absent from school, too," Madison said.

"Maybe they ran away together," Dan joked.

"What if something bad has happened?" Madison said.

"You think too much," Dan said. "Let's just finish feeding the animals, okay?"

Madison and Dan handed out bowls of kibble and refilled water bottles up and down the rows of cages. The front office had gotten busier by now, so Eileen asked Dan to help her out. More animal owners were seated in the waiting room when Madison returned.

"I have to call my mom to come get me," Madison said, picking up the desk phone and dialing.

Eileen was busy helping the owner of a Saint Bernard. The dog had drooled all over everything, making the floor slippery. Dan got a bucket and mop to clean the mess.

While Madison waited for her mom to arrive, she watched a family come into the clinic with their sick parakeet. The little girl who owned the bird was about four, Madison guessed, and she didn't stop crying the whole time she was there. Madison thought it was amazing how close people felt to their pets. But she knew that feeling herself.

Madison said her good-byes to Dan and Eileen and went outside the clinic to get some fresh air, even though every time the air blew, it felt like icicles.

Madison stuffed her hands into her pockets and paced to keep warm. Something was really off the wall in Far Hills these days, she thought. From Mrs. Wing to Aimee, Madison felt way out of the loop.

But Dan was right. She had to stop thinking about it so much.

She wrapped her scarf in a tighter knot against the cold and wished for snow, as she always did.

Chapter 3

Mom made pancakes on Sunday morning, which was the perfect way to start the day. She decorated them with orange smiles, cherry noses, and pineapple eyes, too, just as she had when Madison was little.

Pancake decorating was an "Oh, come on, honey bear, cheer up!" Mom trick, Madison thought, gobbling up the eyes, nose, and mouth before drowning her pancake in syrup—and it was a trick that usually worked.

Today, however, it didn't.

"Do you feel okay, Maddie?" Mom asked. "Want to talk?"

Madison looked down at the table. "I'm just sad about Aim, that's all—and the whole puppy thing. I know it's dumb, but that's how I feel. Sometimes it's like I'm the last person to know stuff."

"I thought your friends told you everything," Mom said reassuringly.

"Me, too. But lately people aren't acting the way they usually do. My teacher even vanished off the face of the earth without telling me first," Madison said.

"Does someone have a case of the winter blahs?" Mom asked. "I get that way sometimes, too. When it's gray and cold outside . . ." She stroked the back of Madison's neck.

Madison poked a fork into her half-eaten pancake. "Maybe a little."

Mom poured herself another cup of coffee and sat down in the seat next to Madison. She had an idea. They could spend the afternoon giving each other beauty treatments. That might chase away the blahs.

First they would heat up water in a pan and give themselves a steam facial. Then Mom would paint Madison's toenails, even though Madison's feet were ticklish. She had bought new nail polish in a Tropical Punch color Madison liked. It would be just like the afternoons when Mom used to let Madison into her closet to play dress-up, only much better. Right now Mom seemed more like a friend than a mom—and Madison liked it that way.

Mom heated up the water and took out her

supply of lotions and creams. Madison got clean towels and then retrieved Mom's bathrobe and slippers. Then she put on her oldest T-shirt. She didn't mind if it got wet or stained. A couple of hours later, they made cocoa and watched TV. Madison felt like a different person.

Since Mom needed to get a little editing work done for her film company, Budge Films, she and Madison ended their day of beauty around three o'clock, with a big hug. Madison headed upstairs to check her e-mail, hoping that Bigwheels—or anyone—had written back to her.

The e-mailbox was packed.

```
   FROM            SUBJECT
✉  FHJH Server     Cancel Download
✉  TheEggMan       The Wall
✉  JeffFinn        Fw: Sounds Good
✉  GoGramma        I Miss You
✉  Bigwheels       Re: When Things Fall Apart
```

The first message was a returned e-mail Madison had sent earlier on Friday, while she'd been at school. It must have gotten held up in the system. She always sent herself a message to remind her of what she had downloaded while at the computer lab. Friday was when she'd done the demonstration for her lab and the wacky substitute, Mr. Franks.

She clicked onto Egg's message next.

29

```
From: TheEggMan
To: LuvNstuff, MadFinn, BalletGrl,
Wetwins, Wetwinz, Sk8ingboy,
Dantheman, W_Wonka7
Subject: The Wall
Date: Sun 5 Nov 11:29 AM
```
Yo I have been surfing online
alldaylong and im telling u the
WALL site is awesome u have to
check it. i feel like i can tell
who is writing what since 1/2 the
postings are from people i know, at
least i think so. Goto the bulletin
board 4 sports and school and dont
forgetGossiP

peace, out, egg

Wow. Everyone really was logging on to The
Wall, Madison decided. She'd have to look at the site
again later on, when she had time to surf from topic
to topic and read the postings in more detail.

She read the third message, a note from Dad.

```
From: JeffFinn
To: MadFinn
Subject: Sound Good?
Date: Sun 5 Nov 12:03 PM
```
Maddie, I have a plan--and I hope
you go along with it. Stephanie's

nephew Kirk is flying in from Texas
for a visit and she thinks we
should all meet up together. He's
just about your age, maybe a little
older. We could go for Mexican and
maybe go to the movies? What do you
think? Let me know.

p.s. What did one Eskimo say to the
other Eskimo? What's an ice guy
like you doing in a place like
this? LOL.

Love you,

Dad

Madison cringed.

Stephanie's nephew?

She couldn't imagine a fate worse than being
forced to sit through dinner with a distant relative
of her Dad's girlfriend. And even though she had
no idea what he looked like or how he acted,
Madison had already decided that Kirk must be a
major dork. Of course, there was the distinct possibility that Kirk wouldn't be a dork. But, Madison
thought, why risk it?

Dear Dad . . .

Madison thoughtfully composed a polite response in her head.

Um . . . dorks are not really in my future. . . .

Madison chuckled to herself and then continued thinking of a *real* response.

Dad, I don't know if I can make it to dinner this week. . . .

What was a really, really, REALLY good excuse?

I have to walk the dog.

I have to wash my hair.

I have to save the world from an alien attack.

Madison giggled.

How *would* she get out of this? More time was needed to come up with the perfect reply. Maybe some kind of attack *was* warranted—like an attack of the sniffles? Dad always listened and felt sorry for Madison when she was sick (or at least when she *pretended* to be sick).

She would call him later to cancel.

Madison hit SAVE and moved on to the next e-mail. Gramma Helen had written to check in. Sometimes she did that on weekends.

From: GoGramma
To: MadFinn
Subject: I Miss You
Date: Sun 5 Nov 2:57 PM
_____
Your mother sent me a copy of
your last book report, Maddie, and
I was so impressed. I went to the
library to get myself a copy of
Lois Lowry's *Number the Stars*, too.

I am just reading it now. The
librarian there asked me if you had
read *Love That Dog* or anything by
Sharon Creech. Have you? I think we
should exchange reading lists. I
like your books better than
the romance novel I read last
week.

I dug out some old photos from
a drawer the other day and found
one of you sitting on your
grampa's knee. He looks so happy.
I will send it to you. If only
I had a scanner, I could do
it right now. Can't have
everything!

It's been snowing here all day.
This is some cold weather.
I miss you very much. I need to
plan a visit soon.
All my love,

Gramma

Madison hit SAVE and put Gramma's e-mail into
her special file. Some notes were worth saving.
Gramma Helen's were always in that category.
There was one e-mail left.
The best she had saved for last.

From: Bigwheels
To: MadFinn
Subject: Re: When Things Fall Apart
Date: Sun 5 Nov 3:10 PM

Before opening the e-mail, Madison looked at the time it had been sent: 3:10 P.M. Now it was 3:13. Was Bigwheels still online . . . right now? Madison typed a quick Insta-Message. She couldn't help but grin when, checking her buddy list, Madison found Bigwheels online—and ready to talk.

<Bigwheels>: OMG I miss uuuuuuuu
<MadFinn>: how's life?
<Bigwheels>: BORING school is a drag
    we have these standardized tests
    all week ICK
<MadFinn>: I think we have ours 18r
    in the yr
<Bigwheels>: How's HART--LOL--u
    haven't mentioned him lately did
    he get ugly or something
<MadFinn>: VVF--no he's ok (and
    still a QT) but I haven't seen
    him much mostly seeing annoying
    boys instead!!!
<Bigwheels>: did u & Aim make up?
<MadFinn>: NY
<Bigwheels>: Don't be mad about the
    puppy thing does she know ur mad?
    DON't BE MAD!!!

\<MadFinn\>: \<GRRR\>

\<Bigwheels\>: make up soon she's ur BFF I got into a scream match with my friend April and then we didn't talk for like a year it was so bad

\<MadFinn\>: well me and Aim didn't scream im just avoiding her

\<Bigwheels\>: BTW I totally have checked out The Wall

\<MadFinn\>: whaddya think?

\<Bigwheels\>: look @ the postings under Gossip--juicy

\<MadFinn\>: what kinda stuff?

\<Bigwheels\>: not like bigfishbowl.com at all

\<MadFinn\>: y not???

\<Bigwheels\>: one girl wrote this nasty thing that's obviously about someone who thinks they're friends only she's only being fake--how mean is that?

\<MadFinn\>: sounds mean

\<Bigwheels\>: I have 2 go out w/my dad and mom and sister and bro it's my sister's birthday this wkend

\<MadFinn\>: have a good time :>)

\<Bigwheels\>: O&O

\<MadFinn\>: yeah bye

\<Bigwheels\>: *poof*

After signing out of her e-mailbox, Madison wanted to rush online to visit The Wall, but she remembered a geometry homework assignment she'd forgotten to finish for Monday. So she logged off and quickly opened a file before cracking the books.

In the Loop

Rude Awakening: I'm so not in the loop. I'm just loopy.

That's what Mom says when she gets real busy with film work, "I'm loopy!" like her head's spinning.

This week my head is DEFINITELY spinning.

Dan tells me to chill out about the whole puppy thing, but I just can't let go of it. I really and truly feel hurt and I can't stop being a little bit mad at Aimee. Besides, I got a million e-mails tonight, but not one from Aimee. What's that about? Since when doesn't she call me on the weekend?

And where is Mrs. Wing? Doesn't anyone else want to know?

Is it so wrong to want information or to want to be included in things?

Oh, maybe Mom is right. I do have the winter blahs.

At least my toenails are in the pink. Hot Pink Tropical Punch.

Chapter 4

Unfortunately, Madison fell asleep on Sunday before she could finish her math homework. So on Monday before class she hid out in the girls' room with her notebook, desperately writing answers on a page as fast as she could. She didn't want her math teacher, Mr. Sweeney, to see her. She didn't want *anyone* to see her.

The bathroom was an ideal hideout. As it turned out, it was also an ideal place to hear people whispering things that Madison was probably not intended to hear.

As she huddled in the stall, two girls walked inside and turned on the water faucets. Madison guessed they were washing their hands and putting on makeup, that kind of stuff.

Madison recognized a certain pair of platform shoes and denim, flared pants, but it wasn't until she heard the voice that Madison knew for sure who was in the bathroom with her: Poison Ivy Daly.

Ivy's voice was like fingernails scratching on a blackboard.

"I don't see what the big deal is," Ivy whined. "I mean, I didn't really *fail* the test. I only got a D, you know. Mr. Danehy is such a pain."

Joan her drone agreed. "Science is so dumb anyway."

"And if that stupid twit Madison had just sat differently, I could have cheated off her paper, anyhow," Ivy said. "She's such a goody-goody."

Madison's jaw dropped. She wanted to barrel right out of the stall and clobber Ivy over the head with her notebook.

Instead, she took a deep breath and tried to remain perfectly still. She balanced her books on her lap and pressed her feet into the door to keep from falling over.

"Can't you just protest the grade?" Joanie asked.

"Why bother?" Ivy groaned. "Mr. Danehy said I could make up a lab or something and get the D up to a C. That's all I need to do. I'll just ask Hart to help me."

Madison bit her tongue. Ivy liked Hart, too, which meant that they fought over everything—including their crush.

38

"You'll pass science," Joanie said.

Ivy laughed. "Who really cares? I can always copy Madison's lab notes anyway. I do it all the time when she isn't looking."

Madison's eyes bugged out of her head. She'd had no idea that Ivy had been copying her answers all year. Ivy really *was* evil.

Thankfully, Ivy and Joanie disappeared out of the bathroom just as the class bell rang. Ivy never knew Madison was there, and Madison was able to regroup before heading off to class.

Sort of.

The truth was, she couldn't stop thinking about Ivy all through math . . . and then social studies . . . and English, too.

Madison couldn't focus. Everything blurred together on the pages of her textbook. Even a school assembly couldn't shake her thoughts. Near the end of the day, when Principal Bernard and Assistant Principal Goode called everyone together for the second-to-last period, Madison spent the whole time keeping her eyes out for Ivy. She was so preoccupied that she nearly crashed into Aimee and Fiona on the walk there.

"Maddie!" Aimee cried as soon as she saw her. "Whoa!"

"Oops," Madison said, just managing to sidestep her BFFs.

"Gee, are you still sick?" Aimee asked. "Your

mom said you were sick this Saturday when I came over to see you and . . . she *did* tell you I came by, didn't she? I was kind of hoping you might e- me or something, but I didn't hear from you."

"Yeah, *yeah*." Madison recovered. "Mom told me. But, you know . . . I was taking some medicine . . . so I don't remember exactly when she told me. But she definitely did."

"Oh," Aimee said, sounding disappointed. "I wanted to walk the dogs together. Next time, I guess."

"Next time?" Madison said. "Yeah, sure."

Madison seemed a little distant, which registered on Aimee's face.

"Well, fine," Aimee said, looking a little dejected. She walked ahead of Madison and Fiona. "I forgot something. . . . I'll be right back."

Fiona, who had been just listening, looped her arm around Madison's. "Hey, Maddie, what's going on?" she asked softly. "Is something wrong?"

"What do you mean?" Madison asked, feigning indifference.

"What's up with you and Aimee?" Fiona asked. "You seemed so strange, the way you talked to her. . . ."

Madison shrugged. "What way did I talk to her?"

"*That* way. Like you're mad."

"Fiona, why would I be mad?" Madison asked. It was too embarrassing for her to admit the truth about the puppies and about lying to Aimee that she'd been sick. Madison looked away. She scanned the room for Mrs. Wing, but her teacher wasn't sitting with the other teachers.

The auditorium filled up fast with classes from grades seven, eight, and nine. People in the room hooted and hollered and tried to get settled. Spontaneous assemblies like this one in the middle of the day were always disasters. Fiona and Madison chose seats near the middle of the room. They saved one for Aimee and another for their friend Lindsay Frost. Egg, Drew, and Hart lined up one row ahead of them.

"Hey, Finnster!" Hart turned to her and said hello.

Madison smiled and said hello, quickly looking around to see if Ivy were anywhere nearby. She hoped Ivy had seen Hart's friendly greeting. . . . but Ivy wasn't looking. She was too busy talking to her drones. The enemy sat two rows away, between Joan and Rose.

The noise in the room sounded like buzzing flies. Madison listened as kids all around her talked nonstop about one thing: the Internet. Everyone who was gabbing gabbed about The Wall. Madison could even hear Ivy Daly's voice above the din.

"Check out the gossip page . . . on The Wall," Ivy said. "There was this post . . . 'best-looking classmates.' . . . I think we should do that, too."

Madison strained to hear.

"Why don't you post . . . message about . . . like Hart?" Rose's words came through the din.

"Shut up!" Ivy cried, much louder this time. She gave Rose a smack on the shoulder.

Madison wished she could hear *everything* they were saying. Sometimes eavesdropping seemed like a bad idea, but not when it came to Ivy.

"Attention, students. May I have your attention, please?"

The microphone onstage clinked and Principal Bernard stepped forward to speak.

"Thanks for coming in today. We have great news. Far Hills Junior High has been chosen as a blue-ribbon school in our district. This is the third time we've received this great honor. . . ."

Ms. Goode led the room in a round of applause.

Principal Bernard smiled and introduced a city representative who presented him with a plaque for the cabinet in the main lobby. Madison knew exactly where it would probably hang. The city rep didn't say more than three words: "Congratulations, Far Hills."

Then Ms. Goode stood at the podium and read through a quick list of clubs in the school that were sponsoring special activities in the coming week. Ski Club was planning a trip. Art Club was painting a mural in one of the boys' locker rooms.

"Okay, students, you may return to class," Ms. Goode said.

And just like that, almost before it had even begun, the assembly ended. The whole announcement hadn't taken more than five minutes. The room broke out in a roar.

"Wait! That was *it*?" Aimee cried. "That can't be it. This is the dumbest assembly I've ever been to. I missed dance class for *this*?"

"Couldn't they just have sent around a note or said all that stuff on the loudspeaker?" Lindsay asked.

This place is surreal, Madison thought.

Just as quickly as everyone had been called together, they were hustled out of the auditorium and sent along to their two remaining classes for the day. Madison had computer lab and science. She crossed her fingers that Mrs. Wing would be back in the classroom.

But when she arrived in the lab, Mr. Franks was sitting in the chair at the front of the room. Today, he was wearing blue horn-rimmed glasses. Madison guessed he must have them in every color of the rainbow.

Thankfully, the funny substitute didn't ask Madison to do any additional, attention-drawing demonstrations on the school Web site. Instead, he spent the class time showing students tricks on PowerPoint. He didn't seem to care that half the kids in class said they didn't know PowerPoint.

Madison spent most of class thinking about what

she'd overheard that morning. Ivy Daly was the world's biggest cheater. Maybe it was time for Madison to confront Ivy in science class? Maybe it was time for Madison to stand up to Ivy in front of Mr. Danehy and Hart and everyone else at FHJH?

No, I can't do that, Madison thought. Ivy was the one who was causing trouble, not her.

I need to catch her in the act, Madison said to herself. She would get her "revenge" when she could catch Ivy red-handed—and not a moment sooner.

Of course, no revenge-planning mattered much on this particular day, since Ivy never even showed up at science class. Madison did her lab assignment alone.

Since Ivy wasn't there, Madison felt a bit more courageous about approaching Hart on the way out of class. Sometimes, she walked up to him easily, as if they were good friends (which they were), but other times, she just clammed up.

Today was a clam-up day.

The moment Hart made eye contact, Madison looked the other way.

As Hart and the other guys exited the room, she lingered behind to help Mr. Danehy put away the lab materials. By the time she left the classroom, the final bells of the day had rung and most of the kids had rushed to their lockers and bolted out of the school. Even Madison's BFFs were long gone. Aimee had gone to her dance lesson. Fiona had headed for indoor soccer. Lindsay was working on the Art Club project, in a basement studio.

The winter blahs were coming on strong again. Mom had been right.

Madison stuffed homework, textbooks, and everything else she needed into her orange bag. Then she pulled on her winter coat, scarf, and gloves.

"Maddie!" someone yelled down the hall. Madison spun around to see Dan, out of breath, running toward her.

"Hey, Dan," Madison said. "What's up?"

"I am so glad I caught you," Dan cried. "I have something really, really important to tell you."

Madison's mind danced. For a moment she wondered if maybe Dan had discovered the tricks Ivy was playing in science class. She'd have a witness to Ivy's evil actions. But that didn't really make sense. How would Dan have known any of the facts about Ivy's spying on Madison's notebook? She'd only just found out about it.

"What is it?" Madison asked.

"I finally found out what happened to Dr. and Mrs. Wing," Dan said, clasping his hands together. "My mom told me last night."

Madison felt a teeny knot in her tummy. "Told you? What? What happened?" she asked. "Is it bad?"

Dan smirked. "You are *so* NOT going to believe this."

 Mrs. Wing

My computer teacher is a mom!!!

Mrs. Wing had a baby. Well, she *got* a baby. She and Dr. Wing adopted a baby last week. And she missed school suddenly because that's how it works. They got a last-minute call to go pick up the baby and had to rush into New York to get her at the airport. Some social worker brought her on a plane all the way from Korea. Oh yeah, it's a little girl. A little girl! I don't know her name yet.

Wow. Dan was right. I can't believe it.

Of course, once again, I was one of the

LAST to know. But at least this surprise is too good for me to mind.

Rude Awakening: Good news comes to those who wait . . . and wait . . . and wait. . . .

What I don't understand is how Mrs. Wing and Dr. Wing could keep quiet about this. Amazing! I couldn't keep news about having a baby a secret! I'd be blabbing it all over.

One thing's for sure: Mrs. Wing will be the BEST mom on the planet. Except for mine, of course.

Madison sat back and reread her file. A wide grin spread across her face.

What better way to celebrate the news than to post an announcement on the computer? Madison punched in the Web address for The Wall. She could share Mrs. Wing's baby news with all the other kids at FHJH on one of The Wall's bulletin boards. That way, it would seem as though maybe *she* knew something before everyone else knew. Of course, she wouldn't come right out and use names or anything. That was against bulletin board rules. Kids were allowed to use only first initials and abbreviations.

Madison scanned the list of topics once again and selected GOSSIP. That seemed like the right category for her news. This was *good* gossip. She carefully composed her message in her head as a long list of postings showed up on-screen. Some of the subtopic categories were the same as they had been the last time she'd checked. Others were new.

```
HOT TOPICS: GOSSIP
What should I do???        7
Friends-n-enemies         12
Shut Up                   10
The big joke              41
Random thoughts            8
Oh, Baby!                  4
Big newz                  11
Hotties                    9
```

Madison tried to figure out which category would be the best one to use for her posting or if she should create her own. "Big newz" was an obvious first choice, but then Madison spotted "Oh, Baby!"

Her jaw dropped when she saw the four simple postings.

```
Posted by:   Fairyprincess
Date:        5 Nov
Message:     OMG our teacher had a
baby and no one even knew that is
so wild I think maybe she has a
double life or something LOL :)
```

```
Posted by:   Chatter106
Date:        5 Nov
Message:     so what who cares
```

```
Posted by:    Fairyprincess
Date:         5 Nov
Message:      Ur not supposed to be
here if u don't want to post for
this topic so get lost u probably
don't even go 2 my school FHJH so
there!!! :)
```

```
Posted by:    LunaWow
Date:         5 Nov
Message:      I go 2 FHJH who r u
talking bout??? Mrs. W.?
```

Madison scrolled back to make sure she'd read the messages correctly. Had Fairyprincess really written *FHJH*?

That has to be Far Hills Junior High, Madison thought. What else could it be? And it can't be a coincidence that LunaWow wrote "Mrs. W.," can it? That has to be Mrs. Wing. Who else?

From under her bedroom desk, Phin nuzzled Madison's bare foot with a cold, wet nose.

"Oh, Phinnie, how could those kids have learned about Mrs. Wing before me?" Madison wailed.

"Brrrrrrrrrrroooooooof," Phin snorted, rolling back over onto the carpet. He wasn't particularly interested in the Internet right now. He wanted to be tickled.

"I wonder who these posters are?" Madison said aloud, punching the BACK button on her

49

browser. She returned to the main menu of Gossip.

This time, she selected a different category, called "Hotties," that had nine postings. Maybe she could uncover the identity of Fairyprincess with a few more clicks.

```
Posted by:    KraZeeCat
Date:         5 Nov
Message:      who r the cutest class-
mates in ur class? Remember NO last
names or they will pull your post
```

```
Posted by:    99QTPIE
Date:         5 Nov
Message:      no one in my class is
cute . . . they're all ugly LOL and
the only cute guy is pretty MEAN so
that makes him ugly IMHO anyhoo but
I do like a guy in the other jr
high named Carlo
```

```
Posted by:    *-Lashida-*
Date:         5 Nov
Message:      my bf Rob I am trippin
4 him
```

```
Posted by:    KraZeeCat
Date:         5 Nov
Message:      I forgot to say mine:
josh, josh, josh, josh, josh, and
oh yeah, josh!!!!!!!!!!
```

Posted by: Whassup00
Date: 5 Nov
Message: 1. H.! 2. Geoff S. (@ the high school) 3. Craig B. (@ a different school) 4. Zach (from camp) 5. TJ (my friend's bro) 7. Luis (neighbor) 8. Tommy (sometimes) 9. this guy J & R & I saw walking his dog on the street--I wish I knew HIS name! :)

Posted by: Jamie-12
Date: 5 Nov
Message: no offense to any guys out there but the guys in my class are GROSS and so immature

---

Posted by: BalletGrl
Date: 5 Nov
Message: actually I like this guy Ben but no one really knows so shhhhhhhhhhhhhhhhhhh I should not have written that

---

Posted by: Wetwinz
Date: 5 Nov
Message: of course someone who has been flirting w/me a lot wink wink can u guess who? *G*

Posted by: BBCool
Date: 5 Nov
Message: I have a big crush on
my friend's brothr but she doesn't
know it yet b/c I think ths other
guy likes ME so weird what should I
do? I'm at Kennedy Jr Hi in case u
were wondring

Madison laughed out loud.

BalletGrl? Wetwinz? That *had* to be Aimee and Fiona! Those were their screen names from bigfish-bowl.com. Of course, Madison was in the middle of being mad at Aimee, so she couldn't exactly call her up to confirm the identity. But she knew it had to be her friends.

How could Aimee have written about liking Ben, the smartest guy in their class? Aimee must have figured that no one would see it or guess that she'd written it down, Madison thought. And Fiona hadn't revealed the name of her crush, because, of course, that would have been a dead giveaway. Madison didn't know too many other kids anywhere who could possibly be named Egg.

Unfortunately, Fairyprincess was nowhere to be found on "Hotties." And when Madison scanned "Big newz" and "Shut Up" and "Random thoughts," she came up empty then, too.

By now the sky outside Madison's window had

turned blacker than black. There weren't a lot of stars out tonight, because of cloud cover. Madison picked up Phin and sat by the window, watching the red and white lights of cars on the street.

She imagined Aimee sitting in her room at home, too, typing online and surfing the pages of The Wall. Or maybe Aimee and Fiona were chatting. Madison felt a pang. In a matter of moments, she decided to stop being angry and start talking again. It was hard to be mad at BFFs for longer than two days.

Phin yelped as Madison dumped him onto the floor and dashed downstairs. She grabbed the portable phone and dialed the Gillespie house.

"Hello, Mrs. Gillespie?" Madison said sweetly. "Is Aimee there?"

Mrs. Gillespie called out to her daughter and then proceeded to quiz Madison about home, school, and the other details of her life: "How's your mom? How's your dad? How's Phin?"

Finally Aimee picked up the extension. "Hello?" she said.

"Aim?" Madison said tentatively as Mrs. Gillespie got off the line. "It's me. I was just calling to see what you were doing."

"Nothing," Aimee said, her voice seemingly a little distant. "What are *you* doing?"

"I was just on The Wall," Madison admitted.

Aimee's end of the line was silent. Madison wondered if maybe Aimee were now mad at *her*.

"I saw what you posted," Madison said, trying to break the silence. "That's pretty funny. . . ."

"Don't laugh!" Aimee cried into the phone almost immediately. "Fiona dared me to write that, and we were just goofing around. And once you send a message, you can't retrieve it or change it. It's there forever. So I couldn't take it back. Oh, my gosh, I am so embarrassed—"

"Aim, it's okay. I'm sure I'm the only person on the planet who could guess that you wrote what you wrote."

Aimee's end of the phone was silent again.

"Aim?" Madison asked gently. "Are you there?"

"I'm a little confused, Maddie," Aimee said. "Fiona thinks you were mad about something, and I didn't know you were mad. You could have told me before you just stopped talking to me."

"Huh?" Madison said, trying to play dumb. But then she confessed everything. "I was mad about Blossom, that's all. I was mad about the puppy thing."

"The puppy thing?" Aimee asked.

"I thought you always said Phin would be the one to have pups with Blossom. Not some strange basset hound in a kennel somewhere," Madison admitted.

"*That*'s why you weren't talking to me?" Aimee said.

Madison grumbled, "Uh-huh. That's why I didn't call or e-mail or anything."

Suddenly Aimee seemed to be holding back the giggles.

"Why are you laughing?" Madison asked, a little offended.

"Maddie!" Aimee gasped. "I told you that about the puppies when we were in, like, fourth grade! And besides, my mom and dad are the ones who decide who Blossom will have puppies with, not me. And they want basset hounds, not some mix of pug and . . . Maddie, can you imagine what Blossom and Phin's babies would really look like?"

"Yeah, I guess," Madison mumbled. "I never really thought about that part. Smushed faces and floppy ears. That would be weird. . . ."

"Oh, Maddie . . ." Aimee said.

"Oh, Aimee . . ." Madison said.

Both friends breathed a sigh of relief.

"I'm sorry you were upset," Aimee said. "I hate it when you get mad at me. I never know what to say."

"I'm sorry, too," Madison said. "Hey, Aimee. You know what? I found out something really secret today. I've been dying to tell you."

"You mean about Mrs. Wing?" Aimee said.

"You know?" Madison cried. "About her adopting a baby?"

"Yeah, I just found out tonight. My brother Roger knows some guy who works down at the animal clinic, too. Remember?" Aimee said.

Madison sighed into the phone.

"Are you okay?" Aimee asked, picking up a lingering distress signal.

"I just—I just—" Madison stammered. "I just wish I had found out before everyone else, that's all."

"Maybe she'll bring the baby into the computer lab and you can play with her," Aimee suggested.

"Maybe," Madison said. "Hey, do you want to walk to school together tomorrow?"

"Sure," Aimee said. "I'm gonna wear this new sweater my grandmother knit for me. It is so beautiful—you are totally going to want to borrow it."

"I'll meet you out in front of my house at the usual time," Madison said.

"Thanks for calling, Maddie," Aimee said. "I'm glad you're not mad anymore."

Madison hung up the phone gently, trying not to think too much about the fact that she had been so far out of the loop once again.

Brrrrrrring!

Madison stared at the ringing phone before picking it up. "Hello?" she asked tentatively, expecting it to be a call from one of Mom's Budge Films coworkers or one of her latest dates.

"Maddie?" a voice on the other end whispered. "Hey! It's Fiona." Her voice sounded low and serious.

"What's up?" Madison asked, plopping back down onto the couch.

"I was just calling to see if you were okay. You

seemed so out of it at school. I meant to call earlier, but I had to help my dad with this—"

"I'm fine," Madison said, cutting her off. Fiona was playing peacemaker. "And you'll be happy to know that I just got off the phone with Aim, too."

"You did?" Fiona said. "Really?"

"Yeah, we made up. So you don't have to worry anymore."

"You guys talked!" Fiona squealed. "I'm so glad! I was so worried that you guys would be in this feud for the rest of the week or even longer, and I didn't know what to think. I miss it when it's not the three of us BFFs together, don't you?"

"Of course," Madison said. She was relieved, too.

"By the way, I heard some big news," Fiona said.

Madison sighed. *Everyone* had known about Mrs. Wing except for her.

"Yeah, yeah, big news, I know," Madison said. "Mrs. Wing had a baby."

"Huh? What are you talking about?" Fiona gasped. "A baby? She did?"

Madison stopped. "Wait. You didn't know?"

"MRS. WING HAD A BABY?" Fiona cried again. "Oh, wow! That is, like, HUGE news. My news is so little and puny compared to yours. I just found out that the soccer team is moving their practice space. Wow! How did you find out about Mrs. Wing?"

"You really didn't know about the baby thing until I just told you?" Madison asked. "Really?"

"How would I know?" Fiona said. "Did Mrs. Wing call you or something? I know she's, like, your favorite teacher."

"No, Dan found out at the clinic," Madison explained. "Since Dr. Wing works there . . . and *he* told me. They adopted a baby girl from Korea."

"Adopted a baby! That is so cool!" Fiona said. "Oh, wait Maddie—my mom just came into my room. I have to get off the phone and finish the reading homework. I'll see you tomorrow at school, okay?"

"Okay," Madison said. "See you."

As Madison hung up the phone this time, she smiled so wide her face hurt.

Fiona had *not* heard the news. What a relief! Madison wasn't the very last of the last to know. She looked over at the clock on the wall.

As of that very moment, Madison was definitely back in the loop.

Chapter 6

"Maddie!" Fiona called to Madison in the hallway at school on Tuesday morning. "You have to come quick! Do you have your laptop?"

"Yeah," Madison replied. "I have it right here—"

"Well, bring it!" Fiona said. "I'll be just outside the school yard doors. Hurry."

Fiona shuffled away. Madison hurried to dump her science books into her locker and retrieve her laptop. It was a free period at school. Madison didn't understand why Fiona was spending hers in the school yard. The only kids who spent recess out there played ball.

"Fiona?" Madison said as she stepped outside the doors. It wasn't very cold out, which was strange for November. Some days could be blustery, but today it was almost warmish with the sun shining.

A group of guys were playing kickball in the corner of the yard. Other kids were sitting around, too—more kids than Madison had expected to see. She guessed it was mostly eighth- and ninth-graders, because she didn't recognize many from her class.

"Maddie! Over here," Fiona cried. She was sitting a few feet away, leaning against a brick wall.

Lindsay was with her. She was crying.

"Lindsay? What's wrong?" Madison asked, looking worried. "What happened? Are you okay? Are you hurt?"

"Sort of." Lindsay sniffled. "But I don't want anyone to see me like this."

"What happened?" Madison asked.

"Open your laptop, Maddie," Fiona requested. "Lindsay has to show you something."

"You can go online?" Lindsay asked. "You have one of those cards?"

"Sure," Madison said, booting up her laptop. Soon she was pressing all the keys to log on to the Internet. Fiona asked her to open the home page for The Wall.

Then Lindsay leaned in and hit a few keys.

A screen appeared that showed postings for one of the subtopics under Gossip. Madison had never visited this board before. It was called "Friends-n-enemies." She scrolled down to one particular posting.

Lindsay pointed to the screen. "Read it," she said.

Posted by: LoVeBuG
Date: 6 Nov
Message: there is ms. fatty in
my class and she is SOOOO fat that
she cant even go 2 regular camp LOL
she has to go to FAT CAMP and she
walks around with a dumb black
haircut & purple backpack that looks
like she should be in first grade
LOSER!!! I feel bad 4 her yah right
NOT FHJH would be better w/o her :)

"Wow," Madison said, rereading the message. "That's so harsh."

"That's so ME," Lindsay said.

"Get out!" Madison said. "How do you know that? It is not—"

"Maddie!" Fiona chimed in. "Read it again! Black hair? Purple backpack? FHJH?"

Madison sat there, stunned. "But, Lindsay, why would anyone write this about you?"

Lindsay sniffled again. "I guess I'm just ugly or something."

Fiona leaned in and gave Lindsay a big hug. "You are not," she said, comforting her. "You're beautiful."

Madison scrolled down to see if "LoVeBuG" had written any other messages. The writer hadn't.

"It has to be someone in our class who's writing this," Lindsay said. "I mean, it could be someone in the upper grades, I guess. I didn't know anyone hated me this much."

"Oh, Lindsay," Madison said. She closed her laptop. "We should report this to the Webmaster or something. They can remove the posting."

"I tried that already," Lindsay said. "They said they would look into it. But it hasn't been removed yet. So, obviously . . . they . . . don't . . . care. . . ."

She started to sob again.

"I am totally boycotting that Web site now," Fiona said. "I thought those bulletin boards were supposed to be for fun. They have that announcement at the front about not swearing and keeping it real and keeping it fun."

"But who listens to rules, right?" Madison said.

She surveyed the group in the school yard and wondered who else outside had visited The Wall. How many people from FHJH had seen that particular message? How many postings said such hurtful things about people who didn't deserve it?

"Fiona's right. We should all stop logging on to the site," Lindsay said. She wiped her nose. She kept starting to cry and stopping again.

Fiona rubbed Lindsay's back, and they walked back into the school. The bell would be ringing to announce the next class, and they didn't want to be late.

"I'm not going to class. I'm going to the nurse," Lindsay said.

"The nurse?" Madison asked.

"I want to go home," Lindsay said. "Every time I see someone, I'll think that they're the one who posted that message. I bet it was the guys. I know they make fun of me because I'm overweight. I heard them once."

Madison's mouth opened. "You did?"

"Yeah," Lindsay said. "I heard Hart and Chet talking once about who was the prettiest in our class."

"Hart and Chet?" Madison said.

"What did they say, exactly?" Fiona said with a grimace. "My brother is such a geek. Don't listen to him!"

"I don't remember everyone they were talking about, but I do know they said Ivy was the hottest girl and that some other girls were okay but some were too fat, like me and Beth Sanders."

"Well, Lindsay," Fiona said softly. "Beth Sanders *is* fat. She's huge. She takes up two seats at lunch. You're not fat like that."

"That's not the point, guys," Madison said. She didn't like calling anyone names, not even Beth Sanders.

"Look, I'm just repeating what I heard," Lindsay said. "And it hurt."

"Why didn't you tell us before?" Fiona asked.

"I was too embarrassed," Lindsay said.

"I can't believe it. . . . Hart said those things?" Madison said. "Are you absolutely sure?" She couldn't imagine the love of her life being that cruel.

"Boys can be *sooooo* mean," Fiona said. "And I bet it is totally a boy who wrote that post, too. Some guy is going on the gossip page pretending to be a girl. They don't think we'll figure it out."

That sounded right. It was sneaky, just like some of the guys Madison knew . . . or *thought* she knew. She spent the remainder of the afternoon thinking about which guys might have written the message. Every class became an exercise in elimination, based on what the guys were wearing, what they said, and what they did. Egg and Drew became prime candidates, because they were so smart about computers. But it was hard to imagine Madison's best guy friends saying anything mean about Lindsay. They liked Lindsay.

Then again, Egg had been one of the main people who kept telling Madison to log on to The Wall. . . .

In the world of gossip, *anyone* was fair game.

By the time school was through, Madison was no closer to finding her suspect. She had named and eliminated almost every guy she knew—and a bunch she didn't know, too. Meanwhile, Lindsay's mother picked her up and took her home.

Aimee lost it when she heard about what had happened. "I hate that stupid Wall!" she cried. "I'm never going on it again, and you shouldn't go, either!"

Madison knew the truth. They would all huff and puff and complain about how terrible it was to post gossip. And *then* they'd each go home that very night and check the next postings on the gossip page—just in case something interesting came up. At least, Madison would check the site. These days, she was finding it harder and harder to resist.

As Madison left the school building, a car appeared out front, honking at her. It was Dad.

"Hop in! I'm making you dinner at the apartment," Dad said, pulling over to the curb.

Madison walked over alongside the car and yelled into the rolled-down window. "But this isn't our regular dinner night," she said.

"I know," Dad said. "The plan's changed." He came to a complete stop.

Madison was always happy to see Dad, but she groaned at this sudden change of plan. She had been ready to head home, log on to The Wall, and spend the afternoon reading about other people's problems—alone. With Dad in the picture, she couldn't surf the site as she had hoped to.

"Rowwwwwrooooooo!" Phin howled. He was in the backseat, jumping around, his little pink tongue darting in and out. He loved car rides more than anything.

Sometimes Dad "baby-sat" when Mom had to work late. It didn't happen often, but when it did,

Madison usually felt a little tossed around. She understood why Mom didn't like leaving Madison alone in the house all evening, but she didn't know why Dad's place had to be the automatic destination.

Madison slung her orange bag over her shoulder and climbed into Dad's car. They pulled in to his apartment parking lot moments later.

Upstairs, while Dad prepared pasta dinner, Madison sat in the living room, trying to finish up her book report that was due the next day. Phin played with a stuffed bear on the floor. He'd chewed the eyes and nose and was now working on the fuzzy ears.

"Maddie, I meant to ask you, how was that math test you had last week?" Dad asked.

"I'm not doing so good in math right now," Madison said.

"What?" Dad said, wandering into the living room with a spatula in his hand. "But you're my math superstar!" he cried. "You've always been an A student in math."

"Sometimes," Madison said. "I've been having some trouble these days. Just a little. Nothing to worry about."

"Spending too much time on the computer and not enough time finishing up your homework?" Dad asked, tentatively.

"NO!" Madison barked. "I only go on the computer for good reasons. Like my files, which are my journal, basically. I mean, you and Mom always said it would be good to keep a diary, right? And I do homework, like this book report. . . . You know I don't spend too much time on the computer, Dad. And besides, *you*'re always on the—"

"Madison!" Dad's tone got sharp. "Computers are my business!"

"Okay, but what's your point?" Madison said.

"Your mother says you've been logging on to some Web site and chatting a lot," Dad said, squinting a bit, as if he were looking for a little more information than Madison was supplying.

"Bigfishbowl.com, yeah," Madison said. "You know that site, Dad. I've showed you a zillion times. It's where I get my e-mail. Of course, I have to log on to that site. And sometimes I chat with Aimee and Fiona and check out the other new sites. . . ."

"Okay, okay," Dad said, waving his spatula in the air. "But do your homework first, right? I don't like hearing about your having trouble in math. . . ."

"Yes, Dad, I do my work first," Madison said, eking out a little grin.

Dad grinned back and returned to his simmering pasta sauce.

Madison turned back to the laptop screen and stared at the title of her book report. It had only one paragraph following it, and she had to fill four more pages—at least. She closed her eyes and tried to think of words to write.

A few moments later, however, Madison wasn't thinking about the book report at all. She found herself hitting INTERNET CONNECTION on her desktop. Dad was busy in the kitchen, so he didn't hear when the computer whizzed and the Wall home page came clanking onto the screen. Madison followed the prompts directly to the hot topic of gossip and the subtopic "Friends-n-enemies." She reread the post that Lindsay and Fiona had shown her in the school yard that day.

"Excuse me. What's *that*?" Dad said.

Madison jumped.

"Homework, huh?" Dad shook his head. "That's some interesting-looking book report, hmmm?"

Madison didn't know what to say. She didn't even hit the sleep screen on her monitor. She just stared up at Dad, dumbfounded.

"What does that text say? 'Fat camp'?" Dad said, looking at the screen. "'Looks like she should be in first grade LOSER'"? What is this? This isn't an e-mail from one of your *friends*, is it?"

Madison squirmed. "Oh, no, of course not. It's a new bulletin board. Kids post stuff on it. Gossip and stuff. I don't have any idea who wrote this."

"This Web page doesn't sound like you, Madison. Where's the Web site monitor? Aren't they supposed to keep an eye on what's posted on these bulletin boards?" Dad asked.

"Well, this is an unusual post, Dad. It's not like most of them, which are nice and fun," Madison said. She was taken aback by Dad's serious shift in tone.

"Are you defending this kind of talk?" Dad asked. "What else are kids posting here? Does your mother know that the site says these things?"

"Dad, it's not like someone's naming real names or anything. This could be *anyone*," Madison said. She couldn't believe she was defending the negative message that had hurt her friend Lindsay so badly only hours before.

"Let me see this," Dad said, bending over Madison's laptop. She leaned back and let him scroll around. To her relief, he clicked "Sports" and "School" next. There he found a bunch of lame postings about hockey and homework.

"See?" Madison said. "It's not that bad. I told you."

"Hmmm, maybe not," Dad said. "I suppose the Web site has policies about what can be posted."

"Of course!" Madison said. "Most postings are nice. Kids don't want to be mean, right?"

"I don't know about that," Dad said, even more serious than before. "I think kids can be very mean."

Madison tried changing the subject a little bit. "Do you think boys or girls are meaner?" she asked.

Dad chuckled. "You want me to say boys are meaner. But, you know what? I think it has to be girls."

"Daaaaaad!" Madison moaned.

"Seriously, Madison. There was this girl in my seventh-grade class who I remember tortured me."

"Tortured?" Madison asked.

"You bet," Dad said. "Even I was picked on at school."

"Wow," Madison said.

"I know you think the Web site isn't a big deal, but I'm concerned. This is serious. I'm going to speak to your mother about this."

"Mom? No! Do you have to?" Madison said.

"Of course I do," Dad said, his voice unwavering.

Madison sighed. "Okay, I guess it is a big deal. Fine. I'll act more serious about it from now on," she said.

Dad smiled. "Well, don't get *too* heavy on me," he joked. "Why don't you log off for now and come eat?"

Madison took a deep breath. The apartment smelled like tomatoes and basil and cream and garlic. Her belly rumbled like a volcano.

"Do you want salad?" Dad called from the kitchen, where he was finishing up making dinner.

"Sure," Madison said, shutting down her laptop and heading into the kitchen.

Phin jumped up onto one of the chairs and panted for a treat of his own.

Madison broke a bread stick in half and shared it with him.

70

"I'm really sorry about the Web site," Madison said as Dad put a steaming plate of penne pasta in front of her. "You're right. I will be more careful on The Wall. I'll be more careful everywhere."

"I hope so," Dad replied, in a serious voice. "The Internet can be a great place for information and communication. But you need to watch yourself. I don't like the tone on that site. . . ."

"Okay, okay, Dad, no more lectures," Madison said. "Please?"

"By the way, Maddie . . . I can help you with the book report after dinner if you want," Dad added with a wink.

"You can?" Madison cried. "You're the best."

"You only say that because I'm the one feeding you," Dad cracked.

Madison smiled and grabbed another bread stick.

Chapter 7

On Wednesday afternoon, Madison hid in the corner carrel of the library, putting the finishing touches on her book report. Dad had been a huge help. Madison had nothing more to do than proofread the pages and print the report out for delivery to Mr. Gibbons at the end of the day.

She popped her disk into a computer station in the media center of the library and did a spell check on the document. Everything looked good. Then she sent the document to the big printer in the librarian's office.

While she waited for it to print, Madison opened up a file she'd been working on that morning. She was continuing her new file in honor of Mrs. Wing's new baby—and had included a VID (very important document) that had been sent to her *personally* by Mrs. Wing. Well, everyone in class had gotten a copy, but Madison liked to think hers had been a private note.

Mrs. Wing

Update on the baby: Mrs. Wing made contact!!! She sent all of the kids in her special computer lab a group note (I scanned my copy in here). I think she misses us as much as we miss her.

Greetings to all my computer students!

As you now know, my family has a beautiful new addition. My husband and I adopted a baby girl last week. Her name is Phoebe Kim Wing and she's now four months old and as bright as a beam. We couldn't be happier.

I will be out of school for several weeks while we all get used to each other. But I wanted to check in and make sure that you are continuing with your computer work, especially work on the school Web site.

I've spoken with Principal Bernard, who has made arrangements for the substitute, Mr. Franks, to help with the update on the site. Starting Friday, November 10, you'll resume your after-school meetings. Please, everyone, show him that you're working hard. Come to the first meeting on time. It will start after three o'clock, which gives you time to sort your stuff after the last bell. He will help you set up new pages and updates.

And I'll be back very soon—I promise.

Missing you,

Mrs. Wing

Madison hit SAVE after pasting in the scan of Mrs. Wing's letter. She was just about to walk into Mr. Books's office (Mr. Books was the school librarian) to check on her book report printout when someone came up from behind and tapped Madison on the shoulder.

Madison turned around, half expecting it to be Egg or even Dan, goofing on her while she was busy working.

But instead, she came face to face with Fiona.

"Hey, I was looking for you. I need to talk to you!" Fiona whispered.

Madison wrinkled her eyebrows. "Why are you whispering?" she asked.

"I have a secret," Fiona gushed. "And it's a BIG secret."

"Define *big*," Madison teased.

Fiona punched her gently on the shoulder. "Come over here, and I'll tell you," she said, dragging Madison out from the seat near the computer toward two rows of bookshelves in the back of the library.

The two BFFs collapsed onto the floor in the nonfiction section, between *G* and *P*, where no one could hear them.

"Okay, so he finally, really asked me," Fiona said. Her eyes twinkled.

"Asked you? What? *Who?*" Madison asked.

"Egg! He asked me out. For real," Fiona said.

Madison gasped a little. "He asked you *out*? He said those exact words?"

Fiona nodded, giggling. "He wants to go to the movies next week. Can you believe it? I know we're sort of a 'couple,' but this really makes a difference. He said his sister, Mariah, will take us, so I know our moms will agree to the date, because we'll have a chaperone."

"Wow," Madison said. "I can't believe it."

"He just asked me, over by the lockers."

"Double wow," Madison replied. "He asked you right here in *school*?"

Fiona nodded, grinning from ear to ear. "Maddie, I really, really like him so much. And the deal is that Mariah told him that when we get to the movies, she might just let us sit alone anyway. Isn't that cool? I have butterflies in my stomach—I'm so nervous and excited at the same time. It'll be like going to the movies *alone* together, don't you think? What do you think will happen?"

Madison sat back, nestled in between the two bookshelves, and took a deep breath of stale library air. It smelled like old books there. Fiona's news actually made her *dizzy*.

"It'll be like going alone on a real date," Madison said. "Lucky you."

Fiona bowed her head. "Are you okay with all this? Because I know you and Aim have always had this thing where you felt weird about me and Egg liking each other. . . ."

"No, I'm really happy for you, Fiona. Does Aimee know?"

Fiona shook her head. "Not yet. She's meeting with a teacher right now. You're the only person on the planet I've told. You can't tell anyone else."

Madison crossed her heart. "I won't tell a soul. I swear."

"Oh, it's almost time for the next class. I just couldn't wait to tell you. I was ready to explode!" Fiona said, standing up and grabbing her book bag. "I'll e- you later, okay?"

"Later," Madison said, waving good-bye. She was slower to get up off the floor and grab her stuff.

Brrrrrring.

The class bell rang. It echoed in the library. Madison smoothed out her pants and tugged at her woolly sweater. She felt warm, so she stopped to pull it off and tie it around her waist.

"So you're here, too, huh?" said a voice from behind Madison as she stood readjusting her clothes. Poison Ivy snapped her gum.

"Oh, hello, Ivy," Madison said coldly. She turned to walk away, but Ivy stood directly in her path.

"On the way to science class?" Ivy asked.

Madison rolled her eyes. "Yes, aren't you?"

"Of course I am. But I need to borrow your notes before class. I didn't have a chance to finish one of my labs," Ivy said.

"Ha!" Madison laughed out loud. "Sure, you didn't."

"Excuse me?" Ivy snarled.

"I bet you didn't even *start* the stupid lab assignment," Madison said.

Ivy looked a little flustered. "What's your problem?

You're my partner. You're supposed to help me."

"No, we were supposed to work *together*," Madison said.

"That's what I'm talking about," Ivy said. "Are you deaf?"

"No, I'm not deaf," Madison said calmly. She was enjoying watching Ivy get all worked up. Usually, Ivy was the better bully, but Madison liked those rare moments when she felt in control.

"You obviously don't know the meaning of the word *homework*, Ivy," Madison said. "It means you actually have to do work, at home."

"Well, YOU obviously don't understand what it means to be *partners*, Madison," Ivy whined. "It means that occasionally you show me your notes. I would do the exact same for you."

"Yeah," Madison mumbled. "If you ever took notes."

Ivy's jaw dropped. "Excuse me?"

"Look, Ivy, I have to go," Madison said. "Why don't you just ask Mr. Danehy for help?"

"Whatever!" Ivy fumed. She turned on her heel and walked away.

Madison slung her orange bag over one shoulder and watched Ivy disappear through the library doors. Then Madison followed, at a safe distance, so she wouldn't have to encounter Ivy again until they were safely inside Mr. Danehy's science classroom.

Unfortunately, the girls' lab seats were right next

to each other. It was pure torture; it was sitting in the lap of the enemy, Madison thought. Worst of all, Ivy and her drones whispered all during class and Madison just knew they were gossiping about *her*. At one point, they passed a note over to Hart and he laughed out loud.

Madison hoped the note didn't say something bad about her. She hated to think of Hart laughing at her expense—right in front of her!

When the final bell rang at the end of the school day, Madison was eager to get out of the building and away from Ivy. Aimee was still in her dance class and Fiona had indoor soccer, so Madison considered walking a little bit of the way with Egg. She didn't want to head home alone again. But walking with Egg was tricky. What if Madison were to let it slip out that she knew the real deal about Fiona and the movies?

The air outside was crisp—a real November day. Madison walked home alone quickly. Mom's late afternoon meeting was bound to run even later, so Madison was responsible not only for walking the dog when she got home but also for getting the food out for dinner.

She heard Phinnie scratching at the door and the floor, panting fast as she walked up the porch steps. He knew she was coming.

"Helloooo, Phinnie!" Madison called, fumbling for her house key. She kept the key tied to a string that she knotted inside her orange bag. It rattled in the lock and Phin let out one long "Rowrrooooooooooooooooo!"

He practically knocked her over as he jumped up to say hello.

Madison grabbed the worn leather leash and attached it to Phin's collar. She made a loop around the neighborhood, passing Aimee's house first and then turning onto Ridge Road, which passed Fiona's house. Madison giggled to herself as she thought about Fiona's upcoming "date" with Egg. She imagined him buying Fiona's ticket, saying nice things, and then reaching out in the darkness of the theater to hold her hand. . . .

Ewwwwww!

Madison shook off the thought immediately. No matter what, she couldn't imagine Egg romantically—in any context, especially not with her BFF.

Some thoughts were just off-limits. This was one of them.

Phin soon seemed eager to head back home, so they hustled back. The streets weren't busy this afternoon. Madison passed people racing home from work and walking their dogs, too, but since it was cold outside, she didn't see too many kids playing or riding bikes. As she approached the Finn house, she waved to a neighbor out fixing a shingle on the side of his blue house.

By the end of the walk, Phin's paws were cold. He

raced back up the steps quickly, pulling Madison behind him.

Once inside, she dumped her coat in the hallway and turned on the radio. Helping get dinner ready required good music. Madison flicked on the Top 40 station and listened for Jimmy J and the Dudes, one of her favorite bands. They didn't come on after three songs, so she turned the radio back off.

Mom had left a note with detailed instructions on what to prepare. Madison needed to chop lettuce and tomatoes for the salad. She needed to turn over the chicken that had been marinating all afternoon. She also needed to shuck some corn. Even though it was out of season, Mom had found some salt-and-sugar corn, the yellow-and-white-mixed kind that always tasted so sweet in the summertime. It was nice to have it for a treat on a cold day. Madison hated peeling "hair" off corn, but she'd do it anyway.

Before making any dinner preparations, however, Madison decided to make a cup of instant hot cocoa and watch some TV. She could procrastinate with her homework, since Mom wasn't around. Phin didn't seem to care. She flopped in front of the tube and channel-surfed her way through an hour.

After four-thirty, Madison finally turned off the television set and started chopping vegetables.

She was standing over the garbage can shucking an ear of corn when the phone rang.

Madison picked it up. "Hello?" she said, expecting to hear Mom's voice on the other end.

"Maddie? Is that you?" the voice said.

It was Fiona. She sounded upset.

"Fiona?" Madison asked, concerned. "Is something wrong?"

Madison could hear Fiona taking a deep breath on the other end. She sounded as though she'd been crying.

"Maddie, I can't believe you!" Fiona cried out.

"What happened?" Madison asked.

"You promised you wouldn't tell!" Fiona said.

Tell *what*? Madison was confused. "Fiona . . ."

"I thought you were my friend," Fiona said. "How *could* you?"

Madison felt her stomach flip-flop. She dropped the ear of corn onto the kitchen floor, nearly bonking Phin on the head.

"Please tell me what's wrong," Madison pleaded with her friend.

"Why don't you read The Wall?" Fiona said. "You'll see what I'm talking about, Maddie. You'll see."

Fiona hung up.

Chapter 8

"Hello? Hello?"

Madison clicked the receiver twice, but Fiona was gone.

She considered dialing her BFF back again but decided she'd better check out The Wall first.

Phin chased Madison around the house as she retrieved her orange laptop and bag and set up her computer on the kitchen table. She quickly logged on to the Internet.

The Wall home page came into view.

Madison punched a few keys, looking for whatever it was that had gotten Fiona angry. But she didn't see anything. Then she surfed to the topic "Friends-n-enemies" once again.

That's when she saw the message.

```
Posted by:   MF13
Date:        8 Nov
Message:     some secrets r way
2 hard 2 keep even about my
friends F.W. sez its all good but
she and W.D. probably want to hook
up @ the movies next week I know
it what a j-o-k-e they are so NOT
innocent :)
```

Madison swallowed hard. "'What a j-o-k-e,'" she read again, aloud. "'They are so NOT innocent.'"

She couldn't take her eyes off the "posted by" screen name: MF13.

Those were Madison's real initials *and* her lucky number.

Anyone reading that post would have thought *she* had written it. That was what Fiona had thought.

Madison clicked around to see what other messages lay hidden on the site, but she couldn't find anything—and certainly not anything about Fiona or Egg.

After she'd carefully looked around, Madison picked up the phone and dialed the Waterses' house. Fiona answered.

"Fiona," Madison said softly. "I read that message in the Friends-n-enemies section of The Wall. I can't believe you think I wrote that."

"What else am I supposed to believe?" Fiona asked. "It says your name right at the top—and you told me you would keep a secret. I feel so hurt, Maddie. How could you do this to me?"

"Wait a second!" Madison said. "I didn't do it. I didn't do *anything*. I haven't even been around my computer since I was at school, *before* you told me about the date with Egg. And I never would have told anyone. You know that!"

Fiona grumbled on the other end. "Yeah, well . . . who else could have done that? I told you that no one else knew."

"Are you sure you didn't tell anyone else?" Madison asked.

"What? You don't believe me?" Fiona cried.

Madison thought for a moment. Someone else must have known—somehow.

"Egg knew!" Madison said aloud, without really thinking.

"Huh? You think *Egg* posted that on the Web?" Fiona said. "That is so mean. How could you think that? Why would he do that to me?"

"Wait, wait," Madison said, backtracking. "I didn't mean he posted it. I mean . . . maybe he told someone else who posted it. You told me, so he probably told Drew or Hart or someone, right? Maybe he didn't keep it quite as secret as you did."

Fiona paused. "What are you talking about?"

"What if Egg told Chet?" Madison suggested. "Isn't your brother always trying to get you into trouble?"

"Chet?" Fiona said. "Yes, he is always trying to get me into trouble, especially with my mom. So what?"

"And you're always telling me how obnoxious he is," Madison said. "He wouldn't care about hurting your feelings, would he?"

"No, Chet couldn't have done it," Fiona said. "He's a dork, but he's not a mean dork."

"But he admitted that he likes visiting The Wall, didn't he? And he knows me and my lucky number, so he would know all the information to make up a fake-o screen name." Madison wanted to find a reason to make Fiona think someone *else* was guilty of the posting. She had to find out who had done this!

Fiona's end of the phone got very quiet.

"Do you really think it could be Chet?" Fiona asked. "Because he has done worse things to me in the past. And he might know about the date from Egg, that's true. Wow, I just never expected . . ."

Madison chimed right in. "I bet he won't admit it, either," she said. "Like, if you ask him, he won't say he did it. He'll say someone else, like me, did it."

"Maybe you're right," Fiona said. Her mind was working fast now, Madison could tell.

"I swear up and down and all around, it wasn't me who posted that message, Fiona. I would never break a promise to you. I would never tell one of your secrets," Madison said.

"I know," Fiona said. "But this is a little hard to believe."

"Are you still mad?" Madison asked.

"Well . . ." Fiona sniffled a little. "I just feel so embarrassed. And if Chet did write this, then he'll show it to my mom, and she probably won't let me go on the date now. And I know he'll show it to her, because he's always going on to these bulletin boards now with the other guys."

Madison began to feel a little better that Fiona's suspicions were no longer directed at her.

"What if you're right, Maddie?" Fiona said. "Does that mean Egg told Chet? Maybe I shouldn't even go on a date with him, now."

Madison didn't know what to say. By successfully shifting suspicion from herself to Fiona's twin brother, Chet, she'd made Fiona doubt the one guy she really liked—Egg.

"Don't cancel your date," Madison said finally. "You were so excited about it this afternoon."

"I'm not so excited anymore. I'm embarrassed," Fiona admitted. "Maybe Aimee will know the right thing to do."

"Maybe," Madison said.

"You're the one who should be really mad at

Chet," Fiona said. "Why did he pick your name to sign the e-mail? That was the meanest part of all. I think you should come over right now and we can yell at him together—"

"Let's wait," Madison said, holding her breath. She didn't want to pick a fight with Chet until she had all the facts. Things felt a little out of control.

"Okay, we'll wait. I'll talk to you more in school tomorrow," Fiona said. "Thanks for calling me back. I feel a little better. I'm mad at my brother now, but at least I don't have to be mad at you. I hate that feeling."

"Me, too," Madison said.

After hanging up the phone, Madison collapsed back into the kitchen chair and stared at the bulletin board message, still glowing on her laptop screen.

Someone wanted to make Madison look like the bad girl.

They'd succeeded—even if it was just for a little while.

Madison logged off The Wall and moved into her e-mailbox. There were no e-mails from Gramma or Dad in there to cheer her up. In fact, there were only three e-mail messages, and Madison couldn't identify the senders of any of them, so she hit SELECT ALL and then DELETE.

Then she opened a new e-mail to send to Dan.

From: MadFinn
To: Dantheman
Subject: The Wall
Date: Wed 8 Nov 5:58 PM
_____

I have an important favor to ask. I
tried calling you @ home. R u still
@ the animal clinic with your mom?
Things must be crazy there for u 2
stay so late. So here's my deal: do
you or any of the guys @ school
ever play pranks online? I'm talking
mainly about Chet and Egg and Drew
and maybe Hart. I know u guys like
having fun and goofing on the
girls, but would one of the guys
ever do something that can actually
be categorized as MEAN?

Let me know ASAP. It's totally
important. I can explain more l8r.

Maddie

No sooner had Madison hit SEND than she got an
Insta-Message back from Dan. She leaned back from
the kitchen table, surprised.

<Dantheman>: whassup

Madison typed a response, and she and Dan continued with a virtual conversation.

89

\<MadFinn\>: hey ur online?

\<Dantheman\>: @ the clinic but doing homework while Mom files

\<MadFinn\>: THIS is homework? LOL

\<Dantheman\>: what do u mean play pranks?

\<MadFinn\>: like posting messages on a Web bulletin board that aren't real

\<Dantheman\>: Maybe if it's funny

\<MadFinn\>: even if it hurt someone's feelings?

\<Dantheman\>: Maddie, I think ur losing it. Why do u keep asking me all these bizarro questions? GOIA!

\<MadFinn\>: I'm asking b/c you'll tell me the truth & I trust you

\<Dantheman\>: Well I know 4 sure Egg would never do that

\<MadFinn\>: Y

\<Dantheman\>: No one would really do that Maddie it's uncool

\<MadFinn\>: have u ever made up a screen name for yourself

\<Dantheman\>: >=] who hasn't

\<MadFinn\>: I never did

\<Dantheman\>: yeah well ur perfect HA HA

\<MadFinn\>: VVF

```
<Dantheman>: I gotta go Mom needs
   help with the kennels a cat's
   loose bye
```

Madison typed "*poof*" and the chat with Dan disappeared. She pictured him chasing one of the orange-and-white-striped kittens through the back rooms of the clinic.

She opened NEW MAIL next and typed in her key-pal's screen address.

```
From: MadFinn
To: Bigwheels
Subject: Fake Names and Other
Tragedies
Date: Wed 8 Nov 6:13 PM
```
I am in the middle of a muddle. My BFF Fiona thinks I squealed on her big secret. My friend Dan thinks I'm paranoid. And I think I'm being set up. Well, it's just a hunch--1daful.

This all has to do with that new bulletin board, The Wall. I know you told me you saw it this weekend. Have you been on it during the week? For some reason, I can't stop logging on. Every time I go on the site, though, it seems like

something bad happens to one of my
friends. So far two friends saw
messages posted that were totally
about them--and were super mean. And
one of the messages makes it look
like I'm the one who wrote it
because it says MF13 at the top.

Why can't I just log off and stop
looking at the site? Can I convince
my friends that I haven't done
anything wrong?

Write back soon.

Yours till the wall flowers,

Maddie

As Madison hit SEND, she heard a key in the front
door. Phin dashed into the living room.

Her Mom was home.

Madison yanked her laptop out of the wall
where she'd had it plugged in to recharge the battery. Then she shoved it into the case and put it
under the kitchen table. By the time Mom strolled
into the kitchen, Madison was sitting there looking
angelic, chopping a pepper.

"Hey, honey bear," Mom said, not noticing a
thing. She reached inside the refrigerator for a can

of soda. "Sorry I'm late. These meetings go on and on and on. . . ."

Madison looked up from the chopping board. "I still have a little bit to do," she explained, pointing to the vegetables that were in their plastic supermarket bags.

"Oh," Mom said. "Did you turn over the chicken?"

Madison gritted her teeth. "Um . . . I think so."

To her relief, Mom seemed distracted. "Oh. Good," she said, opening her soda and taking a big gulp.

"So, how was your meeting?" Madison asked.

"This movie we're financing is one big headache," Mom said. "I think I may have another meeting next week, too. You may have to spend some nights with Dad. Is that okay?"

"It's cool," Madison said. "I don't mind."

Mom came over and kissed Madison on the top of her head. "I don't know what I would do without you, honey bear," she said.

Madison shrugged. "You're the only one who feels like that today," she quipped.

But her mom didn't hear her. Looking into the refrigerator, she debated aloud the question of whether they should have frozen fries or potato flakes with the chicken.

Chapter 9

"I believe you!" Aimee said emphatically.

She threw her hands around Madison and shook her friend's shoulders playfully. The two friends sat in the locker room, getting dressed for gym class.

"I just don't understand how Fiona could even think I would tell anyone a secret. You've known me forever, Aim. You know I wouldn't do that, right?" Madison said.

"Maddie," Aimee said gently. "You need to chill out. Fiona was only mad for five minutes. And she isn't mad anymore."

"I know I shouldn't go on The Wall," Madison said. "But it's hard to stay away. I just want to peek and see what other people are writing. Don't you?"

94

"Yeah, I guess," Aimee admitted with a smile. "But not if it's mean."

Madison nodded, agreeing with her friend.

Meanwhile, she was thinking ahead to the next time she'd have a chance to go online.

"What else is new?" Madison asked, switching subjects.

"The kennel owner found a mate for Blossom. Oh, doesn't that sound strange?" Aimee chuckled. "But we're going this weekend so the two doggies can meet."

"And mate," Madison joked.

Aimee laughed. "I hope my mom lets us keep one or two of the puppies."

"She'll never let you—"

"Oh, wow, Maddie! I almost forgot! You have to let me tell you what happened in my studio class yesterday. . . ." Aimee said.

"What?" Madison asked.

"My teacher lost it," Aimee said.

"What do you mean, she lost it?" Madison asked.

"I mean she got super mad at me and everyone else in class. She threw this fit about how none of us practice as hard as we used to. . . . and how we can't expect to be good dancers if we don't try harder . . . and how we're just wasting her precious time. Everyone was so shocked. She's never said or done anything like that before."

"It sounds awful," Madison said.

Aimee started to giggle. "Yeah, it was."

"So what's funny about that?" Madison asked.

"It's funny because . . ." Aimee said. "She said all that stuff, and *then* she pulled me aside later and told me that none of it really had to do with me. She told me I was the most improved in the class. I think I may even have a chance of getting a LEAD in the next production."

"Get out!" Madison squealed. Getting a lead as a seventh-grade dancer was a very special honor. "You're a star!"

"I hope so!" Aimee said. "Of course, I have to get my favorite leotard patched first. I tore this huge hole in it yesterday." She gave Madison a special big BFF hug.

"Thanks for understanding about Fiona," Madison said, giving Aimee a squeeze.

As soon as she'd spoken, Fiona appeared inside the locker room.

"What are you guys talking about?" Fiona said, raising an eyebrow.

Madison turned and threw her arms around Fiona, too. "I was just telling Aimee how bad I feel about what happened on The Wall. I'm so sorry."

"It's okay," Fiona said, smiling. "I think you were right about my brother. When I confronted him about The Wall this morning, he acted suspicious. *Very* suspicious."

"Boys stink," Aimee said.

Madison held her nose. *"Peeeeuuuuw."*

The three BFFs laughed. The bell rang for gym class to begin.

"Wait!" Madison said. "I just have to put on my sneakers."

"Meet us inside," Aimee said, running ahead into the gym with Fiona.

Madison pulled on her sneakers and knotted the laces twice. She hated her gym shorts as much as ever, particularly today, because they were riding up on her butt. Even worse, it was colder than cold inside the locker room, so she had goose bumps up and down the backs of her legs.

"Aimee! Fiona! Wait up!" Madison called out, jumping up and down to keep warm. She turned the corner and entered the gym.

"Okay, girls," the coach said, clapping her hands together for order. "I want to pair you all off for volleyball."

Madison tugged at her shorts. She liked volleyball better than most sports, except when she served. It always left a welt on her wrist, because she hit the ball the wrong way.

Coach Hammond asked everyone to pair off with the person nearest to her. As usual, Madison happened to be standing right next to Ivy.

Grrrrrrrrrrr, Madison thought.

"Nice shorts," Ivy said, pointing. "Is that your idea of a fashion statement?"

Ivy was wearing the exact same type of shorts, but they looked a lot better on her legs, for some reason.

"Yeah, well . . ." Madison didn't know how to respond. She wanted to trade partners and she wanted to trade partners, *now*.

"I can't believe I always get paired off with you." Ivy groaned.

"That makes two of us," Madison said, glancing around. Across the gym, under the basketball net, she saw that Fiona and Aimee were happily joined at the hip. They gave Madison a little nod as if to say, "Sorry! Don't hate us!"

"I despise volleyball," Ivy snarled.

Madison rolled her eyes. "You just despise everything and everyone," she blurted out.

Ivy stared, stunned. "Excuse me? You are so rude!"

Coach Hammond blew a whistle and asked the class to split up and practice their volleyball drills in pairs. Since Ivy didn't even bother to grab any equipment, Madison took a new volleyball from the bin. She wondered if anyone would notice if she threw the ball hard at Ivy's head.

"This is gross. I just did my nails!" Ivy said, holding her hands out in front of her.

Madison gazed up at the large, white clock on the wall and started counting the minutes until the gym class—and her gym partnership with Poison Ivy—would be over.

It didn't happen soon enough.

* * *

Arriving home after school later that day, Madison found a note on the hall table.

Maddie,
    Sorry! Another meeting called @ the last minute! There's a can of soup on the counter and salad in a bowl in the fridge. Have some supper if you get hungry. Otherwise, I should be home after six-thirty and we can eat then.
    Don't spend too much time online, okay?
Love,
Mom

Madison crumpled up the note and yanked a fat, gray book, *Math Made Easy*, out of her bag.

After a little practice in and out of school that week, she was finally getting the hang of positive and negative integers. For some reason, she got confused when she had to subtract a negative number to find the value of *x*. This particular day's math work sheets still showed a bunch of scratch-outs and scribbles. At least, she finished it early.

When she returned from taking Phin for a walk, Mom was *still* not home. Madison could think of only one other thing to do. She pulled out her laptop. Mom had warned Madison not to go online too much, but she couldn't stop herself.

The Wall was waiting.

Each visit to the site was like being inside the world's biggest vacuum cleaner. Madison selected the topic gossip and WHAM! She was sucked in.

Fortunately, the first thing Madison noticed was that the post about "fat camp" had been removed. Lindsay's campaign to the Webmaster obviously had been a success.

Unfortunately, the message from MF13 was still there, glaring at Madison with its flashing yellow letters.

But then Madison saw *another* message, which had been posted earlier that day.

And it had the SAME stolen screen name.

```
Posted by:    MF13
Date:         9 Nov
Message:      A.G. is such a geek she
thinks she can dance who is she
kidding? I know 4 a fact she wears
ripped leotards and dance teacher is
ready 2 KICK HER OUT of class for
being a showoff she will NEVER get
a lead even tho she thinks she is
all that :)
```

Madison sat back, staring at the monitor.
A.G.?

She wanted to cry. Those were Aimee's initials. And the information about ripped leotards confused her. Who was writing these messages and signing Madison's name? Madison wished she could pretend that MF13 didn't exist. Her lucky number was ruined forever.

At the very least, Madison hoped that there was a good chance Aimee wouldn't even see the posting. Maybe Madison could campaign, as Lindsay had done, to have this message deleted, too.

She quickly logged off the site and opened a new file.

 Off the Wall

Rude Awakening: I thought posting on The Wall would be fun, but I can't believe *anything* I hear by word of mouse.

This Web site started out as something good, but it took a major left turn. Who's sending messages and signing MY name?

First I thought maybe it was one of the guys. Chet seemed like the candidate for Most Guilty. He bugs Fiona all the time. It made sense that he would write that message goofing on her big date.

But then Dan told me that that didn't seem like Chet and I agree. Even if Fiona drives him crazier than crazy, would Chet really resort to total, cruel sabotage to get back at her? Why would he pick my name to do it? He knows Fiona would never really believe *I* wrote those words.

Nope, it's not Chet. It's not Egg, Hart or Drew and definitely not Dan either. Which leaves the nastiest person I can name.

Poison Ivy, of course.

Who else has a reason for making *me* look bad and getting revenge on my friends? Who is always lurking around me when my BFFs are telling me their secrets? She must be listening in on my conversations. *That's* where she gets the information about Fiona's date and Aimee's leotards ripping. How else could anyone know those things?

This gives me just one more reason to hate the enemy.

So, now what do I do?

Dingdong.

Madison craned her neck to be able to see in the direction of the front door. She expected Mom, but Mom had a key. She wouldn't have rung the doorbell.

Who else could it be?

"Maddie! Are you in there?" a voice called out.

Madison groaned.

Aimee.

That's who was outside again, just like the other morning. Since Aimee had only just returned from dance class, maybe she hadn't seen the posting. Madison hoped she hadn't.

"Hey, Aim," Madison said as she opened the front door slowly.

Aimee faced her from the front step, bouncing on her toes like a boxer. Aimee's lips were pursed.

"I thought you could keep a secret!" Aimee said.

Madison frowned. She knew that tone of voice. "I can," she replied.

"Been on The Wall lately?" Aimee asked.

"Well—" Madison stammered. "Not really . . ."

"So how did my confession to you today turn into public news?"

Madison gulped. "What are you talking about?"

"Are you still mad about the puppies, or what?" Aimee cried.

"No, I—" Madison didn't know how to answer. "It's just that—"

Aimee simply continued talking. "I really think that is just so ridiculous, and you shouldn't have to make stuff up online or create dumb lies. I don't understand you at all, Maddie. Why do you have to keep going on The Wall anyway? It's just not nice. I thought we were best friends."

"We are!" Madison said.

Aimee made a face. "You're different," she said bluntly.

Madison crinkled up her nose, confused. "What do you mean?"

"Ever since you've been going online on that bulletin board, you've been different. I can't explain it—" Aimee said.

"I swear, Aim," Madison said. "I didn't make anything up. I didn't post any message. . . ."

Aimee's jaw dropped. "Are you joking? Someone else posted all that stuff about me being a bad dancer and a faker? No one—and I mean *no one* else—knew about my leotard being ripped, Maddie. Only you. And we were totally alone in that locker room talking."

"You don't know that for sure," Madison said. She remembered seeing Ivy right after they'd spoken. "I think someone else was there."

"Well, I think that you've flipped out or something," Aimee said. She was letting her temper flare. Her arms were waving wildly as she talked.

"Aim, why would I say that stuff?" Madison asked. "I don't lie. And why would I want to be mean to you?"

"Oh, come on, you have lied before. What about that time in second grade when you told me that you hadn't gotten invited to Miranda Day's birthday party, when you really had?" Aimee said, crossing her arms in front of her chest.

"But I only told a teeny lie then, so you wouldn't feel bad," Madison responded. "I can't believe you even remember that. . . ."

"All I know is that, first, there were those

messages about Fiona . . . with secret information that only you knew. . . ." Aimee said.

"It was *one* message," Madison corrected her.

"And now there's a message for me! That's TWO!" Aimee said. "And they're from the same sender—who just *happens* to pick your screen name! How can you explain that, Maddie?"

"I don't know," Madison said. "I can't explain it."

"Well, I think you were goofing around, and you wrote that stuff, but you just forgot what you wrote, and you didn't think that maybe it would actually get posted forever and ever into infinity. . . ." Aimee's face looked all puffy now, as though she were about to start crying. Madison had never seen Aimee look so upset.

"Aimee?" Madison pleaded. She wanted to cry, too. "How can you think I would do this? You said you believed me when we talked before."

"Yeah, I did believe you. *Before* this," Aimee said. She spun around and grunted all the way down the steps.

Madison wanted to run after her, but her feet froze in place.

Aimee turned around again when she reached the last step. "This changes EVERYTHING!" she cried.

With that, Aimee disappeared around the hedges.

From behind Madison, Phinnie barked at his chew toy in the corner of the foyer. It was wedged between the desk cabinet and the wall. Madison gently closed the front door and tottered over to retrieve the toy for him. She was in a fog.

"Roooooooooowf!" Phin barked, as he bit into the toy once again. Madison followed him into the kitchen and collapsed into a kitchen chair.

Why were her hands clammy?

Was there any way to prove that Poison Ivy Daly was MF13?

She was beginning to believe what she'd feared: The Wall was trouble.

And she was knee-deep in it.

Chapter 10

When she walked over to Aimee and Fiona at the lockers on Friday morning, Madison's BFFs barely said hello.

Egg and the other boys were shocked by Aimee and Fiona's icy reception of Madison. They'd never seen their girl friends act that way around one another.

"Whoa!" Egg said to Madison as soon as the other girls walked away. "Fiona says she isn't talking to you. What's the deal?"

Madison frowned. "Oh, Egg, it's too awful to explain."

"Does it have to do with The Wall?" Egg asked. "Because Fiona showed me those stupid post-ings. You *obviously* didn't write them, Maddie. I don't know what her problem is. She's just upset because it said all that stuff about me asking her out."

Madison's face brightened a little bit.

"Would you tell *Fiona* that, please? She thinks that for some strange reason I've turned into Dr. Jekyll and Miss Hyde overnight. She thinks that I've decided to write bad gossip about my best friends. Why would I ever do that?" Madison asked.

"She's angry," Egg said, lowering his voice. "Wicked angry."

Dan and Drew came over and stood next to Egg and Madison.

"What are you two whispering about?" Dan asked.

"The Wall," Madison grumbled. "And my life being over."

"Life is not over," Egg said. "It's all good."

Madison sighed. "That's what you think."

She felt bad, standing there. Days before, she had tried to blame the boys for the bad postings. She'd even tried to get Fiona to believe that it had been Chet who had done the dirty work. Now here she was, and those same guys turned out to be her only supporters.

"Maybe it's all some coincidence," Drew suggested. "And someone else, in a school miles away, has people with the same exact initials doing the same exact stuff."

Madison rolled her eyes. "Oh, yeah, like that's a possibility."

Her stomach flip-flopped again. *Again.* It had been doing a lot more of that lately than usual.

"Well, I have to go to class," Egg said. "Catch you later."

Madison waved as the boys raced off. She coasted along in their downdraft, heading toward science class.

After everything that had happened the day before Madison decided once and for all that she would stop her visits to The Wall. She would stick to Web sites with careful monitors and grown-up moderators that Mom and Dad would approve of. She'd go for gossip-free pages only.

Yeah, right.

Madison was hooked. How could she stop now?

Plus, when she walked into Mr. Danehy's classroom and saw Ivy sitting up on a stool by the lab tables, Madison knew she'd be visiting The Wall again soon. She had to find out the real identity of MF13.

In fact, *was she looking at MF13 right now?*

Ivy was shameless. Madison watched as her archenemy preened and gazed into a small compact right there in the middle of the classroom, puckering her lips, checking for smudged gloss. She fussed with her red bangs a little, too. Poison Ivy had a new haircut. She always had new shoes, new clothes, new something.

The boys in class, including Hart, were goofing off and double checking their science homework. They scarcely noticed Ivy's obvious routine. But Madison couldn't take her eyes off the enemy.

Brrrrrrring.

When the start-of-class bell rang, Ivy's pink mini-compact disappeared back into her pink backpack, and she sat at attention. Mr. Danehy was super-strict about starting class on time. Even Ivy had to obey his rules.

Madison copied down the week's assignment from the board. Mr. Danehy asked the class to write a short, "team" profile about a physical scientist, with ten key ideas and facts.

The whole time she wrote in her notebook, Madison was careful to keep one eye closely on Ivy. If she were going to prove Ivy guilty of the Wall postings, she needed to watch Ivy's every move. Plus, Madison figured Ivy would be copying stuff out of her own notebook as usual. Madison was determined to catch Ivy in that act, too.

"Okay, everyone, I'm rushing a bit today," Mr. Danehy announced to the class. He looked down at his watch. "I have to leave the room for about ten minutes. While I'm gone, I want you to work on two things. First, look over your homework questions from the last class. We'll be collecting and discussing those today. Then I want you to start working on the assignment with your lab partners."

He pointed to the board.

"Follow my directions and feel free to use the science library at the back of the room. I'll be right back."

Mr. Danehy grabbed a pile of folders and disappeared through the door.

Madison glanced back over at her partner. Ivy smiled a fake smile. The *most* annoying of the dozens of annoying things about Poison Ivy, Madison thought, was her unique ability to turn on the charm when she needed something—and then be spiteful a mere five minutes later.

"So, what do we do now?" Ivy asked, acting coy. "I mean, we are partners, right?"

Madison wanted to scream, "NO! I HATE BEING YOUR PARTNER! GET AWAY FROM ME!" but instead, she just shrugged. She needed to play it cool.

"We need to think of ideas," Madison said.

"What will we write about?" Ivy asked. She had no original ideas. In Ivy's plan, Madison would do all the work, starting with their topic.

"I don't know what to write about," Madison said. "Relativity?"

"Oh, that?" Ivy asked. "Is that when some guy dropped apples?"

Madison sighed. "No, that's gravity."

"You decide on our topic, okay?" Ivy said, examining her fingernail polish instead of doing any more thinking. She looked over at her drones.

111

Madison turned to a new notebook page and wrote "Relativity" at the top. "Why don't we look first in the science textbook for some information?" Madison suggested to Ivy.

"But I don't have my textbook," Ivy said, distracted.

"Okay," Madison said, feeling flustered. "Then I'll look."

She flipped to the index and found a chapter on Einstein. While she was reading, Madison had another idea—a better way to test Ivy's sneakiness.

"Why don't you read this and look for other scientists we could write about? I'll go check in the science library at the back of the room," Madison suggested.

She left her notebook in plain view—a tempting trap, she hoped, as she stood up and walked to the back of the classroom. She kept one eye on her nemesis, desperate to catch Ivy red-handed, copying Madison's homework. Once Madison had managed that, she felt, she would be able to confront Ivy about the nasty postings on The Wall. Everything else would fall into place from there!

"Hey, Finnster!" Hart said. He was looking for a book at the back of the room, too.

"Oh!" Madison said, surprised. "I didn't see you standing there." She twisted her body so she could keep watching Ivy, but Hart stood in the way. Madison couldn't see much at all besides his shirt.

"What are you and Ivy writing about?" Hart asked.

"Um . . ." Madison leaned sideways, still trying to see. "I think we're picking Albert Einstein. Although everyone might pick him, so I was going to look around for other subjects. It's good to have a backup."

"I like science when Mr. Danehy's not here, don't you?" Hart said.

Madison nodded. "Yeah . . . um . . . could you move over to your left just a little?"

"Huh?" Hart said, oblivious. As soon as he moved, Ivy came back into view.

But she wasn't looking at Madison's notebook. She wasn't cheating, as Madison had hoped she would be. She wasn't even alone. Her drones had joined her there. They were probably talking about lip gloss, not science.

"By the way, Maddie, Egg told me about what happened on The Wall," Hart said. "That's a huge bummer."

Madison glanced back. "Aimee and Fiona won't even talk to me."

"They'll come around," Hart said. "They're your best friends."

"The truth is, I think someone is deliberately trying to get me into trouble," Madison said, wishing she could name names.

Hart often hung out with Ivy, so Madison couldn't come right out and blame Ivy directly for being MF13. She didn't want to risk getting him mad at her, too. And secretly she wondered if maybe Hart knew more about her dilemma than he was admitting.

Madison wasn't really sure whom to trust or believe anymore. Could she still tell the difference between gossip and truth?

The drones made a beeline for their own chairs when they saw Mr. Danehy stroll back into the classroom. Ivy put away her compact for a second time. Hart and Madison returned to their seats. Slowly, Mr. Danehy started his standard promenade around the room, quizzing science partners and checking to make sure everyone's homework questions were in order.

"What did you find in the back?" Ivy asked Madison, yawning.

"Not much," Madison said. "We should do more research upstairs in the media center, though. Can you go look after school?"

"Me?" Ivy made a face. "Why don't *you* go look after school?" she snarled.

"I have an after-school conflict today," Madison said simply. She didn't feel like explaining to Ivy that she couldn't possibly go to the media center, because that was the day Mrs. Wing had asked students to set aside for an after-school computer meeting with Mr. Franks, the substitute. It was a few hours Madison had been looking forward to all week. Nothing would get in the way of her attending that meeting, least of all some project with Ivy.

"Well, I have a conflict, too," Ivy said. "Like, I

don't do science work *after* school. That's my conflict." She laughed at her own joke.

"Maybe we should each write our own paper," Madison suggested. "I can ask Mr. Danehy if we can split—"

"No!" Ivy interrupted. "Okay, I'll look in the media center. Don't throw a hissy about it. Gosh, you always overreact. What a drama queen."

Madison felt herself grinning *inside*. She'd matched wills with the enemy and won, very briefly. But she'd won. Ivy was backing down. Plus, Madison had actually convinced Ivy to do *work*. Madison figured that Ivy was worried about her bad grades and couldn't risk getting into more trouble in the class.

"We can look online for more information, too," Madison added. "I'm sure you go online a lot, don't you?"

Ivy sneered. "Sometimes," she said. "But I think you'd better deal with that part."

Madison sighed and opened her notebook to the page with the lab homework notes that she had taken. Ivy glanced at it.

"Oh, no," she said.

"What's your problem?" Madison asked.

"I brought the wrong homework," Ivy said.

She had hardly spoken the words when Mr. Danehy came by their lab desk. "Okay, girls, show me your homework, please," he said softly.

Ivy smiled, and Madison thought she even saw her bat an eyelash or two. "Well, Mr. Danehy," she said sweetly. "I left my answers in my other binder, at home."

Mr. Danehy wasn't buying that excuse. "Yes, well, then you will get an Incomplete for this assignment. Your homework does me no good at home."

"But—" Ivy struggled again to explain.

Madison was enjoying the show.

"See me after class, Miss Daly," Mr. Danehy said. He continued along to the next pair of students.

Ivy caught Madison staring a little.

"What are you looking at?" she asked.

"Not much." Madison shook her head.

Ivy smacked her lips and Madison could smell the bubble-gum lip gloss. The rest of the class period passed more quickly. Madison wasn't sure she could sit near the enemy much longer.

As class filed out, Madison bent down to tie her laces and retrieve some papers that had fallen out of her notebook when she'd picked it up. At the same time, Mr. Danehy stopped Ivy on her way out of class, having waited for the other students to depart before he spoke with her privately.

Madison crouched down so she was half hidden behind the science desk. She had to hear this.

"Ms. Daly," Mr. Danehy finally said. "I need to know how you plan to address the issue of your failing grade in this class."

"Failing grade?" Ivy cried. She lowered her voice, and it was hard for Madison to hear much more. But she'd heard enough.

With one move Madison shoved the papers into her orange bag, not caring whether she crushed any of them or not. She slung the bag over her shoulder and sped out of the classroom without being noticed, apparently, by Ivy or Mr. Danehy. They were still engrossed in conversation.

The halls overflowed with students collecting their belongings, getting ready for sports practices and club meetings, and preparing to head home. At one point, Madison thought she spied Aimee and Fiona, together with Lindsay, by the lockers, but as soon as she approached them, they seemed to vanish.

A few moments later, Madison ran into Egg, Drew, and Hart running down the hall. Egg was carrying ice skates.

"Wait! Aren't you going to the computer meeting?" Madison asked. "Mr. Franks is expecting us."

"Can't," Egg explained. "We have to do hockey drills today. We have a match this weekend."

Madison frowned. "You have practice? What about Mrs. Wing's computer lab?"

"She isn't even in school, Maddie," Egg said.

"But we're the students she counts on the most," Madison said.

"She'll never know if we're there or not," Drew said.

"If you guys aren't going," Madison asked wistfully, "who *is*?"

"I know Lance will be there," Drew said. "He doesn't have anything else going on."

Drew, Egg, and Hart all laughed.

Madison groaned. Great, she thought. I get to sit in computer lab with a weird substitute teacher and an even weirder guy I don't like.

"See you around, then," Egg yelled.

Hart waved, too. "Later, Finnster!" he said.

Madison briefly considered heading upstairs to the media center instead of going to the computer lab. Maybe it would be better to do work on her science project instead of working on the school Web site. Did it really matter if she showed up? Mrs. Wing wouldn't know.

But Madison stuck to her plan and headed straight for Mrs. Wing's classroom. She owed it to her favorite teacher to be there—even if nose-picking king Lance would be sitting nearby and Egg and the other guys were no-shows.

She got there fifteen minutes early, so she parked herself at a monitor facing the windows, pulled a small disk out of her bag, and popped it into the hard drive. She had just enough time to work on her own computer file.

A directory appeared and Madison selected the

file she'd marked Gossip. She'd started it that morning at breakfast, before getting the cold shoulder from her BFFs. Madison reread what she'd written so far in her journal file.

 Gossip

Rude Awakening: If you can't say something nicer than nice, don't say anything at all.

This is something Gramma Helen says to me all the time--and she's pretty smart. I know it's important to remember as I try to make amends with Aimee (fingers crossed) today.

Madison continued typing where she had left off.

News bulletin! Thanks to fake gossip, my friends won't even TALK to me. I wish Aimee and Fiona knew that I have not done anything at all. There is nothing worse than seeing them hanging out without me and talking about me behind my back. They don't understand! Of course, I'm not sure I would either, if I were them, would I?

I'm so confused.

If only I could prove Ivy did it!!! That evil girl is driving me up The Wall, literally. I should have suspected her from the start of this whole messsssssssssss

"Whatcha typing?" Lance came up behind Madison. He startled her, and Madison's finger stuck on the S key.

"Something private, if you don't mind," Madison said.

"Really?" Lance said.

"Yes," Madison said, with a blank look. "Can you just leave me alone, please?"

"Oh, sorry, SORRY!" Lance said, putting his hands up in the air and backing away.

Madison was pleased with his response. She'd finally figured out a way to get rid of him. Just say "Go."

She turned toward the monitor once more but then heard someone coming up behind her *again*. Frustrated, Madison whipped around in her chair.

"Lance, can't I just write something—OH!"

Madison stopped in midsentence.

The person standing behind her wasn't Lance at all.

It was Mrs. Wing.

And in her arms Mrs. Wing was holding a precious baby girl.

Chapter 11

"Mrs. Wing!" Madison blurted out, not thinking. "You're here?"

The baby gurgled, startled by the noise.

"Oh," Madison whispered. "Sorry."

Mrs. Wing smiled and gently leaned in to shush the baby with a soft kiss. "I'm so glad to see you, Madison," she said. "I knew you would come to help out with the Web site."

Madison grinned. She had made the right decision in coming.

"Surprised to see me?" Mrs. Wing asked.

"Well, y—yeah," Madison stammered. "Of course. I mean, we missed you so much. It's not the same without you. . . ."

"Would you like to meet Phoebe?" Mrs. Wing asked.

Mrs. Wing leaned down so Madison could look right into Phoebe's little eyes. They were black, with teeny hazel flecks. She had a full head of black hair, too. The baby grinned a gummy grin that sent a stream of drool down the side of her face. Mrs. Wing mopped it up with a tiny blue cloth draped over one shoulder.

"She's so beautiful," Madison said. "She looks like a doll."

Phoebe's skin was flawless alabaster, with thin little eyebrows. As Madison took her tiny hand, Phoebe grasped Madison's index finger with her five little fingers—and squeezed.

"She likes you," Mrs. Wing said. "She doesn't squeeze just anyone's finger."

Madison laughed. She felt her stomach flip-flop again, but in a good way. Phoebe glowed. The baby's gaze never wavered from Madison's face.

By now, assorted other students who were working on the school Web site began to enter the room. Madison's private moment with Mrs. Wing and Phoebe came to an end. But Madison didn't mind. She was just happy to see Mrs. Wing after a long, weird week apart.

"One at a time, please," Mrs. Wing told the kids who were all clamoring to touch the newborn. No one could believe that Mrs. Wing was really standing there with her own baby. Phoebe looked around, unfazed by the crowd.

"How old is she?" one girl asked.

Mrs. Wing explained that Phoebe was four months.

"Isn't it weird just getting a baby overnight?" a boy asked.

"You bet it is!" Mrs. Wing said. "But it's a joy, too. We've waited a long time to meet little Phoebe."

"Aren't you tired?" Madison asked, looking up at her teacher.

Mrs. Wing rolled her eyes. "For sure!" she said with a laugh. "I'm exhausted. But it was important to me to come and visit. I didn't want any students to feel left out or angry about my leaving so suddenly. And most importantly, I wanted you to meet the reason that I left—even if for just a few minutes."

Just then, Mr. Franks came into the room. He'd never met Mrs. Wing in person, so he introduced himself. He was wearing green-framed glasses and looked a lot like a frog.

"I bet you don't get a baby visitor every day," Mr. Franks joked to the kids.

"Neither do I," Mrs. Wing added.

The after-school group laughed in unison.

"She's *soooooo* cute," a girl said, tickling the baby's foot.

"She's so small," a boy said.

"All babies are small," another boy replied. "Duh."

"My cousin had a big, fatso baby," Lance spoke up. "He was so huge, he looked like he was stuffed."

Madison bit her tongue so she wouldn't laugh. Lance always said the wrong thing at the wrong time—but sometimes it was *funny*, anyway.

Mrs. Wing sat in a chair on the side of the room. Kids came over one by one to say their hellos to Phoebe. A few teachers who knew that Mrs. Wing was visiting the school came in to meet the baby, too. Mrs. Wing let some of the teachers take turns holding the baby for a while so she could take a rest.

Madison was impressed to see that Mr. Franks brought in fruit punch and cookies for a snack. It was a nice thing for him to do, especially since he was just the substitute teacher. She poured herself a cup of punch.

"So, how are things going?" Mrs. Wing asked, looking at Madison. Madison saw that Phoebe was nodding off in her stroller, with Assistant Principal Goode watching over her.

"Oh—I'm okay," Madison said. "I guess."

Mrs. Wing poured herself a drink. "You seem a little distracted."

"I do?" Madison asked. Mrs. Wing had always been good at guessing about those moments when Madison wasn't feeling quite herself.

124

"I love seeing all of you again. But where are Egg and Drew?" Mrs. Wing asked, looking around.

"They had hockey practice," Madison said. "They didn't know you'd be here. No one did."

"It was my surprise. This whole week has been a whirlwind for me and Dr. Wing," Mrs. Wing said.

"Does she cry a lot?" Madison asked.

"Not at all, except in the middle of the night, when we need to sleep," Mrs. Wing said with a laugh.

"How come you didn't tell anyone?" Madison asked.

Mrs. Wing took a deep breath. "We didn't want to get our hopes up or talk about it until we knew for sure that we really had a child to call our own."

"Wow," Madison said. "It must have been hard to keep that secret."

"Oh, yes," Mrs. Wing replied. "Especially from you kids! After all, you're practically my family, too."

Madison smiled.

Ms. Goode came over and tapped Mrs. Wing on the shoulder. "You were right. She's fallen asleep," Ms. Goode said. "Sweet thing."

A group of students had gathered around the stroller while Phoebe napped. The baby had a head of wispy hair that was soft as bunny fur, and pink arms and legs that looked like chubby sausages.

"Boooooooh," the baby cooed in her sleep.

Everyone cooed right back.

Ms. Goode snapped a photo of everyone standing together.

"We have to put that one on the school Web site!" Mr. Franks said cheerily. He passed cookies around to the students and teachers in the room.

Madison wondered if Phoebe were dreaming. Her little arms moved a lot when she slept.

"Hey! Maddie!" Egg called out from across the room.

Madison turned and saw Egg and Drew rushing over. They still had half their hockey gear on.

"You boys made it!" Mrs. Wing beamed. "Another surprise."

Egg grinned. "Yeah, of course we made it," he said, tossing his head to the side. Madison laughed at how Egg acted—he seemed smitten in Mrs. Wing's presence. He'd had a crush on her since the beginning of school.

"So we got to hockey practice," Drew explained to Mrs. Wing. "And then someone said you were here. The coach said we should come and say hello for a few minutes, so we bolted."

"I'm so glad to see both of you boys," Mrs. Wing said. She pointed to the baby. "I'd like you to meet Phoebe. She's asleep right now, but—"

"What's that smell?" Egg said.

Drew snorted. "Yeah, what *is* that?"

"Oh!" Mrs. Wing smiled. "Sometimes the baby gets a little gassy after she's been fed. . . ."

"*Ewwww!* Gas me!" Egg cracked.

Madison punched him in the shoulder. "Egg! Don't be such a loser."

Drew snorted again.

"Whoa! She's looking right at me!" Egg said.

Phoebe blinked and rubbed her cheek. She was awake again.

"You probably woke her up because you're so loud," Madison told Egg.

"Why don't you hold her?" Drew said to Egg, joking around.

"Hold her? No way!" he said. "No offense, Mrs. Wing, but I'd probably drop her or something."

"I think it's better if I hold her," Mrs. Wing said. "You boys and girls can just look and say hello from there, okay?"

"She's so little," Drew said. "Ga ga goo goo."

Phoebe's mouth curled up in a smile.

"Did you guys see that?" Drew said excitedly. "She smiled at me!"

Madison and Egg had to smile, too.

"I think you're in good hands with Mr. Franks, kids," Mrs. Wing announced to the entire room. "He says that he'll keep me posted on the Web site's progress while I'm on maternity leave. And who knows? I may drop by for another surprise visit, when you least expect it."

"We'll miss you," Egg said sheepishly.

Mrs. Wing nodded. "I know, Walter," she said. "I miss all of you, too."

Madison could almost see Egg swooning inside at Mrs. Wing's remark.

"Thanks for bringing Phoebe to school," Madison added.

Mrs. Wing said individual good-byes to the Web site helpers. She and Phoebe needed to greet a small group of teachers that had entered the computer lab at the last minute.

Madison, Egg, and Drew each grabbed a last cup of fruit punch on the way out of the room. The boys hurried back to hockey practice. Madison headed for home.

Phoebe's visit had lifted her spirits.

Now she just needed to figure out a real plan for getting her BFFs back.

"I'm home!" Madison shouted as she walked in the front hallway. "Mom?"

"I'm in here, working on a report!" Mom called out from her office.

Madison had already suspected that Mom would be busy working, as she had been all week. Whenever Mom had important paperwork to complete, she always turned her classical music up to full volume.

Madison walked into the office and stood leaning against the door frame until Mom looked over.

"You're home late for a Friday," Mom finally said, noticing Madison.

"They had this surprise party for Mrs. Wing," Madison said. "It was in the computer lab and everyone thought it was supposed to be this meeting with the substitute teacher, but then Mrs. Wing was the one who showed up."

"Oh! Mrs. Wing! Did she bring the baby?" Mom asked. She turned down the volume of her music.

Madison nodded. "The baby's name is Phoebe Wing," she said. "Mom, she's so beautiful. She has this perfect skin and eyes and hair."

"Babies are wonderful," Mom said. She beckoned for Madison to come over so she could give her daughter a squeeze.

"What's that for?" Madison asked as Mom hugged her tight.

"Oh, I don't know," Mom said. "You were my baby, once."

It was a perfect moment for Madison to confide in her mom about all the anxiety she had been having during the week, but Madison didn't know how to bring it up. How could she explain to her mom that she was practically addicted to the gossip page on The Wall?

Mom and Dad and even Madison's BFFs had been after Madison to stop visiting that Web board for days. But Madison hadn't tried to stop. Nope. She'd been on the site even *more*.

"I have homework," she said, pulling away a little. "Gotta go."

"Homework? On a Friday night?" Mom asked.

"Oh, yes," Madison said. "Big science paper, and if I don't start working on it right away . . ."

"Okay," Mom conceded. "Then get going! We'll eat later."

Madison left Mom's office to head for her schoolbooks, but of course, they were the last things she planned on picking up. Instead, she and Phin trotted upstairs to her bedroom, where Madison flung herself across the bed, plugged in her laptop, and logged on.

She resisted The Wall at first and went into her e-mailbox instead. Madison found a lone message waiting there. But it was from the right person.

```
FROM         SUBJECT
✉ Bigwheels   Re: Fake Names and Other . . .
```

Madison breathed a sigh of relief.

```
From: Bigwheels
To: MadFinn
Subject: Re: Fake Names and Other
Tragedies
Date: Fri 10 Nov 11:02 AM
```

OMG IOU a big, huge, MEGA apology so to make up 4 it I will now write u the longest email I have ever, ever written to you, LOL.

Here's what happened. I got the worst flu bug ever and have been in bed for two days. That is why I have not written so please don't be mad at me. My dad would kill me if he knew I was on this computer right now, but he's @ the grocery store so I'm sneaking online. I'm supposed to be sleeping. I hate being sick. I'm way behind in all my classes too, which means next week will be even worse!

So I looked on The Wall and went to that Friends-n-enemies page and it does look like you wrote those messages--the name at least. Who else would use MF13?!! I'm sooo sorry! Still, don't ur friends know u would never do something mean on purpose? Even tho I think they're being wicked unfair, they're prob. just super mad about what was posted.

Did you ever think maybe ur enemy

Poison Ivy wrote it? I know u
didn't say anything about her,
but isn't she always doing mean
stuff 2 u?

I only had 1 weird time in a chat
room when some weirdo asked me if I
was "pretty" and the next thing
they wanted to do was go "private,"
which of course is a big sign that
they're probably a pervert or
something. I told my parents and
they totally freaked. Not on me, of
course. They got all protective and
just told me to be careful when I
go online. My mom monitors where I
go now. BTW, does ur mom or dad
know about this person who is
pretending to be you? U should tell
them!

I would keep talking 2 ur friends.
My friend Zoe says, "Friends
are forever, boys are whatever!"
LOL. Aimee and Fiona know.
Friends always forgive each
other.

Wish me luck this wkend, even tho
I'm sick I need to write this
English paper. I picked *Number the*

Stars like you suggested. What a
good book.
Yours till the cough drops,

Bigwheels, aka Vicki

p.s. 1 more thing I almost forgot
about the person who's posting MF13.
I just noticed they always put this
weird smiley face @ the end of
their posts. Maybe you can ID the
person w/that, like if they use a
smiley with a different screen name
or something. GL!

Madison logged out of her e-mailbox. Bigwheels
was onto something.
Smiley faces!
Madison quickly surfed the bigfishbowl.com site
to see if she could spot other messages where a user
might have used the same symbol—but a different
screen name.

With a little help from her keypal, Madison was
closer to figuring out the true identity of MF13.

Now all she needed to do was to make the phony
user name disappear . . . *permanently*.

Chapter 12

Friday night was unlucky.

Madison hadn't located any smiley-face messages anywhere.

But she hadn't given up.

On Saturday morning, Madison woke up more determined than ever. The more she thought about the nasty messages that had been sent to Lindsay, Fiona, and Aimee, the more convinced Madison was that Ivy was behind the whole charade. While eating her morning bowl of Fruity-Os, Madison got her big, BIG idea.

Revenge.

Of course revenge wasn't something Madison

normally thought about. Gramma Helen, Mom, and Dad all had taught her that revenge was just plain b-a-d.

"Two wrongs don't make a right," Gramma Helen had always said.

But Madison considered the events on The Wall an *exception* to the normal rule about revenge. She needed to brainstorm a master plan. The one way she could get back at Ivy was to give the enemy a taste of her own medicine. She needed to embarrass Ivy way more than Ivy had embarrassed Madison and her friends.

And she knew exactly how to do that.

As Madison's fingertips clicked on the keyboard keys, she remembered Poison Ivy after science class. She could hear Mr. Danehy's words echoing inside her head.

Miss Daly, I need to know how you plan to address your failing grade in this class.

That was all Madison needed to know to launch her plan.

She zipped on to the Wall home page. Once she selected the "Friends-n-enemies" topic, she hit the button that read "New Post."

A blank form popped up.

Madison read the rules in small type that accompanied the form. There were some additional rules that were different than those for the home page for the site.

Without hesitation, Madison started to fill in her
blank form. The first step: to use Ivy's own "fake"
screen name for Madison against her.

```
Posted by:   MF13
Date:        11 Nov
```

After posting the name and date, Madison's fingers tap-tap-tapped faster than usual. She didn't
censor herself.

To get back at Ivy, she needed to *think* like Ivy.

```
Message:    More big newz @ FHJH
this time its I.D. in trouble wow
is she ever. The WITCH is failing
science.
```

Madison couldn't believe what she was typing. It was what she felt—but should she be writing all of this down?

Still, she continued.

```
Yeah I.D. begged Mr. D. to pass
her but he said no way so now the
school is planning to EXPEL her
. . . it is soooo bad
```

Now she was making up facts, but Madison kept writing—faster than before.

```
Not only that but I heard that NO
other school in the district wants
to accept her b/c she has no real
friends n e way LOL in fact there r
no guys who will even look @ her
b/c she dresses
```

"Rowwooo!"

Madison jumped, startled.

Phin was scratching at her foot as though he wanted to go out. She looked down at his impatient little pug face.

"What is it, Phinnie? Can you wait just a sec, please?" Madison pleaded with him. But by now, Phinnie was dancing on his paws.

"Rowwrorororoooo!" he wailed, louder this

time. In dogspeak, that meant, "No, I can't wait. Now, get off the computer. And hurry!"

Exasperated, Madison turned back to The Wall to survey the message she'd written.

Madison was surprised by what she read. She knew she'd gotten a little carried away, but upon rereading her words, she realized that they weren't just mean, they were *meaner* than mean. Even if the posting had been meant to disrespect her greatest enemy in the entire world . . . it didn't feel good once Madison saw those cruel words staring back at her in black and white (well, in blue and orange, actually) on the computer screen.

Madison couldn't send the message.

She quickly clicked on the DELETE key to make the words disappear.

The screen buzzed. Nothing moved.

Hmmm, Madison thought, scanning the entry for another way to delete the words she'd written. She hit SELECT ALL and then DELETE again.

But still, nothing changed. The screen kept buzzing. The cruel words remained.

A moment later, Madison clapped her hands together. Success! The screen finally flashed blue, and she breathed a sigh of relief. The mean message about Ivy had finally vanished for good.

Madison was glad. She didn't really want to get revenge that way.

But a moment later, her relief turned to anxiety.

A new, blinking message on Madison's screen flashed: "Posting Complete."

"Huh?" Madison said out loud. "What does *that* mean?" She frantically looked down at Phin, her eyes darting around the computer screen. "Posting *complete*? What am I supposed to do NOW?! It went through?"

"Rowwrorororoooo!" Phin howled again. He still had to go out, but now he sat down and just panted.

Madison punched a few more keys, hoping the message would return, so that she could eliminate it for good. But nothing returned except the home page for The Wall. Madison gulped.

She had no choice but to check the "Friends-n-enemies" page to see if her posting had landed there.

There it was.

A new posting from MF13—word for mean word.

This one really *was* from Madison.

Madison fanned at her face with a blank piece of paper from her desk. What could she do? She stood up but then quickly sat back down again. Madison needed a plan and she needed one now. How could she have sent the message when she didn't mean to post it? What was she supposed to do to get it back when the rules clearly stated that it was impossible to retrieve a message once it had been sent?

She scanned the room as if looking for ideas. Madison's eyes fell upon a photo of her and

Dad taken the previous summer at the beach.

Dad!

Of course! Dad would have the answer. She would call him now. He'd make everything better again. Dad was a computer genius.

She dialed his number and heard him pick up.

"Dad?" Madison spoke very softly into the phone receiver so her mom wouldn't hear. "Are you there? It's Maddie."

"I know it's you, silly," Dad said. "Why are you whispering?"

Madison sighed. "Dad, I need your help. In a big way. Right now."

"My help?"

Madison quickly tried to explain about The Wall and the postings and the fake screen names, but Dad sounded very confused. She wasn't making a lot of sense.

"So tell me again. Who's MF13?" he asked, for the third time.

Madison wanted to cry. "I don't know who MF13 is, Dad, that's the point. I need to find out the poster's real identity."

"Maddie, honey, can you wait and tell me about this when we meet for dinner tonight?" Dad asked. "It all sounds pretty complicated, if you ask me. And I was just in the middle of an important—"

"I can't wait!" Madison said in a much louder whisper. "Dad, I have to see you right now."

"Maddie, we were going to meet at five. I'm right in the middle of programming something. I have a big presentation next week. . . ."

"I know, I know you're busy," Madison said. "But can't you do your presentation a little bit later? Can't you pick me up a little bit early? Please?"

Dad paused on the other end. "Does your mother know about this strange posting on the Web?" he asked sternly. Madison recognized that serious voice again. She didn't like it.

"No, no. Mom doesn't know. Not yet," Madison said. "I didn't want to tell her before I tried to fix it. . . . Please don't tell her, Dad. . . ."

"Maddie!" Dad said. "We will have to tell your mother, understand?"

Madison said, "Of course," without hesitation. "Can you come get me?" she added. "Right now?"

"Okay, you win. Pack up your laptop," Dad said. "We'll solve this Web site thing together tonight. I'll be right over."

Madison let out a huge sigh. "Thanks, Dad."

"Maddie, be ready in twenty minutes, all right? I just have to drop off a package at the post office first. Oh, and Phin is coming with you, so don't forget to bring his chew toys. I don't want him chewing on my rugs this time."

Madison laughed, relieved. Dad could fix anything. She'd be out of this mess before dinnertime.

Phinnie, on the other hand, wasn't so relieved.

He had been sitting patiently on the carpet while Madison talked on the phone. Now that she had hung up, he was in motion again, scratching at her legs to go for a walk. Madison clipped on his leash and headed outside.

Phin took forever walking around the block. He wanted to sniff everything. Madison practically choked him on the way back home. There was no time for sniffing. She needed to get home. Dad would be waiting.

Mom was so busy inside her office working on the business report that she didn't even question the reason Madison was leaving early for Dad's apartment.

"Have fun, honey bear," Mom said. "Are you two going shopping or something?"

Madison lied. "Oh, yeah, shopping. At the computer store."

"Good," Mom said. "Call me tonight."

Madison leaned over to give Mom a good-bye kiss. She felt guilty for stretching the truth. She felt sneaky for keeping Mom in the dark about the Web problems. Madison vowed never to consider revenge again.

A horn honked in the driveway and Madison heard Dad call out, "Let's go, kiddo!"

Madison grabbed Phinnie and her bag and headed for the car.

She threw her arms around her dad's neck after

climbing into the front seat. "You don't know what a great dad you are," Madison gushed.

Dad winked. "Sure, I do," he said.

Moments later, he pulled into the parking lot at the Stop and Save supermarket.

"Dad! What are you doing? We have no time for this!" Madison cried.

Dad ignored her pleas, however. He needed to buy food for dinner. It only took a few minutes. Soon enough, they were back in his car, speeding off to his apartment in the center of Far Hills.

As soon as they'd emptied the grocery bags, Madison dragged Dad over to the computer. She logged on to The Wall.

"What is this?" Dad asked, looking over the Wall home page. "Isn't this that Web site you showed me earlier this week?" His eyebrows wrinkled together into one.

Madison leaned back in her chair as Dad stood in front of her. His face turned deep pink with sudden anger.

"Oh, Maddie . . . *this* is the Web page you have trouble with? I knew this Web page was trouble. Didn't I tell you to stay away from it?" Dad asked.

Madison didn't answer. She just shrugged.

Dad's voice got even louder. "Madison, answer me," he boomed.

Madison played dumb. "I don't remember, Dad," she lied, for the second time in a half hour.

She hated talking to Dad when he was angry. It wasn't as hard as talking to Mom, but it was close.

Dad read the incriminating post from "MF13" aloud twice, shaking his head both times. Madison was embarrassed to hear her words read aloud. "Do you have to say it over and over?" she asked. "I know it was wrong, and I said I was sorry. . . ."

"I'm just so disappointed in you, young lady," Dad scolded. "What about the Web site's code of honor?" he asked. "Did you read that part?"

Madison shrugged. "I guess," she mumbled. "Look, Dad, I never meant for it to be posted. It was an accident. . . ."

"Maddie," Dad said. "Why would you write those things in the first place?"

Madison had no response. Why *had* she written them?

She quickly surfed around the site to show Dad some of the other negative posts that carried the "MF13" signature, as if showing him the ones that Ivy had written would somehow make things better for her. But Dad wasn't listening anymore. He was too busy trying to find a way to delete the post.

All Madison could do was watch.

Chapter 13

After a half hour of punching keys and surfing the site, Dad finally sent a long note to The Wall's Webmaster. It was a last resort, but it was one Dad thought would work best.

"Well, now the site should delete the post," Dad said. "If you're lucky."

Madison breathed deeply. "I knew you'd help, Dad," she said. "I'm really sorry. . . ."

"Well, let's wait and see what happens," Dad said. "I just don't know what to think about all this, Maddie."

Shaking his head some more, Dad disappeared into the kitchen to start preparations for dinner. He was making a small roasted chicken with baby vegetables, a recipe he'd spotted on some fancy-food channel on cable. Dad was always working on his gourmet cooking skills.

Watching the clock always makes time go slower, Madison said to herself as she watched the second hand on Dad's copper clock tick off the time. She checked her e-mailbox every five minutes, searching for some response from the Webmaster. Why was it taking so long?

Phin curled up in a corner of Dad's living room, chewing on the edge of Dad's rug, as usual. Madison tried shooing him away and tossing him a chew bone, but Phin looked uninterested. The rug obviously tasted much better.

After nearly an hour, Madison was checking her e-mail for the umpteenth time when an e-mail popped up, addressed to Madison with a copy to Dad's e-mailbox, too. Madison eagerly clicked on the message.

```
From: WEBWALL
To: MadFinn, JeffFinn
Subject: Re: Improper Posting
Date: Sat 11 Nov 5:31 PM
```
We have received your e-mail request #17823 and have forwarded it to our customer service area. We understand the urgency in this matter and appreciate your patience as we resolve the problem.

You will receive a detailed analysis of your problem within 24 hours.

Thank you,

Webmaster @ The Wall

"Twenty-four hours!" Madison screeched.

Phin jumped, distracted from his rug-chewing.

"What is it?" Dad cried. He raced into the living room. "Did you scream? Did something happen?"

Madison groaned. "Dad, the site wrote back, but they said they can't respond immediately. It has to be forwarded to some customer service center or something like that."

Dad shrugged. "I figured that might happen. Well, we'll just wait a little longer, then. Have patience, Maddie. We'll get it sorted out."

Madison started to sniffle. She cried only a little at first, but then her tears exploded into one big sob.

"Oh, Madison, now, why are you crying?" Dad asked. He put his arm around Madison's shoulders and patted her back with his other hand, which was still covered by a red, lobster-shaped, oven mitt.

"Dad, I'm so embarrassed. I just wanted to be back in the loop. . . . To be the one who knew stuff before everyone else . . . and now . . ." Madison sniffled uncontrollably. "Now . . . Ivy will probably read what I posted and . . . she'll hate me forever and . . ."

"Wait just a minute, Maddie," Dad said. "I

147

thought you and Ivy weren't friends anymore any-way."

"We're not," Madison gulped. "But . . ."

"Maddie," Dad said in his most serious voice. "You can't keep fighting with Ivy this way. You don't want to be like her. I don't want you to think that being nasty can *ever* make things better. It can't. This whole experience should have proved that. . . ."

Madison hung her head and wiped her wet face. "Why are parents always right?" she said. "And why am I always wrong?"

"You're not always wrong, sweetheart," Dad said. "And as for parents, well . . ." Dad chuckled. "I wish I were always right."

"Well, you're right a lot." Madison sighed.

"One thing I know for sure is that the way to win with Ivy Daly is NOT playing her game or by her rules. Fighting back gets you nowhere with some people, Maddie. Remember that for always."

Dad kissed the top of Madison's head.

Phin trotted past. He sniffed furiously at the air.

"Is something burning?" Madison asked.

Dad took a big sniff.

"Ah! My *Poulet à la Finn* is done!" Dad pro-claimed. He grabbed Madison by the wrist and pulled her up off the sofa. They headed into the kitchen for Dad's feast.

Luckily, dinner went by quickly—and deliciously. The food took Madison's mind off Ivy, The Wall, and her troubles with Fiona, Aimee, and Lindsay. After a dessert of pound cake and fudge, Dad even helped Madison with her math homework. She'd been trying a little harder. Dad noticed the effort.

Before bedtime, Madison was tempted to check her e-mailbox one last time to see if the Webmaster had decided to respond in less than twenty-four hours' time. But she stopped herself. Dad was right. She needed to be patient. Instead of logging on again, Madison curled up in the living room chair and watched the movie with Dad.

The next morning, after a night of good rest, Madison felt more optimistic about the mistakes she'd made on The Wall. She had confidence that the Webmaster would respond and that she would get the negative posting removed, just as Dad had said. Plus, Dad surprised her and took her out for breakfast. Phin stayed behind while Dad took Madison to a diner called Cuppa Joe, up the street from his apartment. They didn't even talk about what had happened.

After breakfast, Madison gathered her stuff together. Dad drove her and Phin back home to Blueberry Street around noon. All Madison could think about was what the Webmaster would say when he or she finally responded to Dad's request. She'd forgotten about one other thing.

But Dad reminded her.

"So how will we tell your mother?" he said, out of

the blue, his hands tapping on the car steering wheel.

"Tell Mom?" Madison said. She didn't turn to look at Dad. "Um . . . I was kind of hoping that we wouldn't have to tell her anything. Since we fixed the problem . . ."

Dad laughed out loud. "You're kidding!" he said. "Oh, Maddie, you are most definitely going to tell your mother *everything*, from the beginning. We had a deal."

Madison sank down into the car seat. The streets dashed by. Why would she tell Mom when she knew Mom would freak? The online nightmare was getting worse by the moment.

"Dad, I think maybe *you* should tell her," Madison said.

"Hmmm," Dad said. "Okay. I'll tell her, but you're going to be standing right there with me."

Madison forced a fake grin. "Whatever you say, Dad," she said.

Phin trotted up the porch steps and entered the foyer with Madison. Dad followed. Mom was surprised to see him there. Usually, when Dad came into the house with Madison, it meant something was wrong, so she suspected the worst.

"Jeff?" she said. "Is everything all right?"

Madison bent down to hug Phin as if he were her security blanket. She wanted this moment to be gone.

"Madison and I spent last night working out some problems she had with the Internet," Dad said.

"Problems?" Mom looked confused. "What problems? Maddie, you didn't tell me you were having problems."

"Mom, it's really not a big deal. I just—"

"Francine," Dad said to Mom. "It seems that Maddie posted a message on one of those popular bulletin boards by accident. The message was not very nice."

Madison cringed.

Here comes the freak-out.

Sure enough, Mom's eyes widened. "What does that mean?" she asked. "Maddie, would you mind explaining this to me, please?"

Dad interrupted. He was trying to keep Mom from getting all worked up. "Francine, I think that I've already covered this with her," Dad said protectively. "The point is that I've contacted the Webmaster to remove the posting. Now I think we have to decide how Madison should be reprimanded for what she did."

Madison's jaw dropped open. "Reprimanded? What are you talking about, Dad?" she said. "You're going to PUNISH me?"

Dad turned to Madison and calmly said, "You didn't think you could do something like this and not suffer the consequences, did you?"

Madison bit her lip.

"Your father is absolutely right," Mom said. "We agreed that the Web was fine to use as long as you didn't abuse your privileges."

Phin scuttled away into the kitchen. He ran away sometimes when people argued or when Madison had heart-to-heart talks with Mom or Dad.

"Shouldn't we wait and see what the Webmaster has to say first, before you decide on some punishment?" Madison asked, feeling very alone.

"Fine," Dad said. "Let's pull out your laptop now and check for a message from the Webmaster."

Madison slowly removed the orange laptop from her bag. The battery was low from all the activity the night before so she plugged it in.

She opened her e-mailbox. Sure enough, the Webwall message she had been waiting to read was there.

```
From: WEBWALL
To: MadFinn, JeffFinn
Subject: Request #17823
Date: Sat 11 Nov 11:54 PM
```

Our team of 24-hour customer service reps has received your e-mail request #17823. Having reviewed the contents of your complaint, we have decided that the improper posting to The Wall by screen name MF13 will be removed immediately.

However, as noted in the rules, the posting violates the honor code of the Web site. Although we do not like to terminate the membership and e-mail address of the user, this member will no longer have access to The Wall. As a result, the member will no longer be allowed to post or read postings on this Web site.

Thank you for your attention to this matter. If you have further questions or concerns, please e-mail us at this address and you will receive further communication within 24 hours.

Thank you,

Webmaster @ The Wall

"Well, I guess that solves that problem," Mom said.

Madison's insides ached. She was embarrassed, angry, sad, and sick, all at the same time.

"I can't go on again? Not ever?" Madison asked aloud. "I'm really off The Wall?"

Dad shook his head. "Guess so. The rules of the site."

"But it's so unfair!" Madison cried. "It was an

accident! I didn't even mean to post those things! I was only writing them because of all the mean stuff that Ivy wrote. It's not fair. . . ."

"Maddie," Mom said calmly. "Why don't you turn off the computer and say good-bye to your father?"

Dad nodded at Mom as though they were speaking in some kind of secret parent code. Even long after the big D, they still shared some moments and secrets that drove Madison crazy. They walked off to the corner of the foyer and exchanged a few private whispers.

Phin trotted back out to give Dad a wag and a lick.

Madison said her good-bye, too.

"I'm sorry I bothered you," Madison said. "I know you had that presentation and all. . . ."

"Try not to worry about that right now. I'll call you later," Dad said, waving to Madison as he went out onto the porch.

Madison waved and stared. She was shell-shocked. After shutting the front door, she and Mom walked into the kitchen together in silence. Mom got Phin a bowl of kibble while Madison poured herself some chocolate milk.

"Rowwwrorororoooo!" Phin pranced around the kitchen, waiting for his food. Madison flipped through a magazine absentmindedly. The kitchen was cold—and not just because of a draft coming from the backdoor.

Dingdong.

Madison looked up, half expecting that Dad was back again. Had he changed his mind about punishment?

Mom went to answer the door.

"Maddie!" Mom called out a moment later. "It's for you."

Madison got up from the kitchen table slowly, sidestepping Phin and his dog dish. She dragged herself back into the foyer. There, in the front doorway, stood Aimee, Fiona, and Lindsay.

"Maddie!" Aimee cried as soon as she saw Madison.

"We need to talk to you, now," Fiona added.

Madison gulped. After all that had happened already this morning, she wasn't sure she could handle more bad news. Had another terrible posting gone up on The Wall under MF13—and were her friends here to blame Madison again? Slowly, Madison walked to the door and prepared herself for the worst.

"Maddie!" Aimee wailed. "We're *sooooo* sorry!"

She threw her arms around Madison and squeezed.

"Huh?" Madison's eyes glazed over. "*You're* sorry? For what?"

"For everything we said," Lindsay chimed in. "For not believing you."

"You're our BFF," Fiona said. "We feel so bad. Oh,

Maddie, please don't be mad. We were just upset about all the postings and—"

"Wait a minute!" Madison stepped back a little. "What are you guys talking about?"

Aimee, Fiona, and Lindsay didn't let Madison get away. They moved in for another group hug.

"Wait, you guys . . ." Madison pushed away from them, because they were squeezing so hard she couldn't breathe. "Please explain what you're talking about."

Aimee started. "We know the truth. We know you didn't put those postings on The Wall. The ones about Fiona and Egg and Lindsay and camp and me and dance class—we know!"

"How do you know?" Madison asked.

"My brother told me," Fiona said. "Well, Chet found out from Hart that Ivy was the one who put all that stuff up there. She claims that she was just kidding around."

"Yeah, *right*," Madison said.

"We should have known it was her and not you," Lindsay said.

"I told you guys I would never have posted mean things. You're my best friends in the whole world," Madison said. She was getting a little choked up. It had been an emotional morning.

"Ivy is such a creep!" Aimee yelled.

Madison nodded. "And she ruined everything."

"No, she didn't!" Lindsay said. "We're back!"

"Yeah, Maddie. We're all still the bestest friends. Don't worry," Fiona said.

"She didn't ruin you guys," Madison explained. "I know you're back. But because of everything that happened . . . well . . . I got into trouble with my parents . . . and I got mad and . . ."

Madison told her friends what she had written on The Wall and how the posting had somehow—mysteriously and accidentally—gone up on the "Friends-n-enemies" bulletin board.

"That stinks! So now your parents *and* the Webmaster say you can't go online anymore?" Aimee cried.

Madison shook her head. "Not online totally—I just can't go on The Wall."

"Well, I don't like that Wall anyhow," Fiona said. "It's mostly mean gossip, as far as I can tell. You know, there are some cool things, like polls, and some of the bulletin boards are okay, but mostly it's people like Ivy, saying mean stuff."

"Yeah," Madison nodded. "I found that out."

"Wow, Maddie, you never get into trouble," Lindsay said.

Madison sighed. "I know," she said.

"I just hope that Ivy saw your nasty posting!" Aimee said.

"Aimee!" Fiona said. "That isn't nice."

"Well, Ivy isn't nice," Aimee cracked. "And it's about time she dealt with the fact that no one likes her. I don't know why the guys even give her the time of day. Fiona, you have to tell Egg to stop talking to her. And why does Hart like her? Does anyone know?"

Madison rolled her eyes. "Because she's pretty," she said.

"That's dumb," Lindsay said. "Boys are dumb."

The four friends laughed.

"So now what?" Aimee asked. "You're not grounded or anything, are you?"

Madison shrugged. "I don't think so," she said. "But I can't exactly hang out right now, either. . . ."

Aimee, Fiona, and Lindsay looked at one another.

"Should we go?" Aimee asked.

Madison nodded. "Maybe. But thanks for coming over. I feel so much better now. . . ."

"You have to e- us later!" Fiona said.

"If I'm allowed online," Madison grumbled. She wondered if her computer privileges would be revoked forever after the Wall incident.

But all of her sad feelings were lightened by a final group hug before her BFFs departed.

And this time, Madison was the one squeezing the hardest.

 My Life

I NEVER thought that I would be the girl who gets into trouble. That was for someone else. And I hate the way it feels. Hate it!

Rude Awakening: Do things get worse before they get better?

Things were bad enough when I got pushed off The Wall. But even though I thought things were looking up when Aimee and Fiona and Lindsay came over to apologize, I was soooo WRONG. Monday, Mom decides that being kicked off The Wall was NOT enough punishment for me. So she decides to also

suspend my laptop privileges for a month. A
month! She says I can check e-mail once a
day for an hour, max. And I have to do it
in the kitchen, when she's there. She's
keeping my laptop--MY laptop--under lock
and key in her desk drawer. It's like being
in prison. Well, at least she didn't take
the laptop away forever.

Anyway, I'm finding time to write in my
computer files at school after classes end
and between periods. Like right now I'm
sitting at a desk in Mrs. Wing's classroom.
It's after 3 o'clock and I'm supposed to be
fixing up the school Web site. (That was
the other condition of my "punishment": Mom
wanted me to volunteer more time to help on
the Web doing GOOD things instead of just
playing games and gossiping.) I'm trying to
add some stuff to the homepage so it looks
flashier. Unfortunately I keep making the
wrong words flash and it looks like

"Maddie?" a voice whispered behind Madison's
terminal. "I didn't expect to find you here today!"

Madison turned around, startled, to see Mrs.
Wing standing in the classroom again! She was push-
ing little Phoebe in her stroller. The baby slept
quietly in a tangle of blue and yellow blankets.

"I thought Web site updates usually happened at
the end of the week," Mrs. Wing said. "I'm surprised
to find anyone in the lab."

"Yeah, w—well . . ." Madison stammered. "I've been coming in more often. Mr. Franks asked for extra help and . . . I'm here every afternoon if I can get here. . . ."

Madison wanted to tell Mrs. Wing the truth about how coming to update the site had been her *mother's* idea more than her own. But she didn't say anything.

"That's nice of you to work so hard," Mrs. Wing said, with a big smile. She looked over Madison's shoulder. "And what are you working on today?"

Madison quickly hit a key on the keyboard and the Web site (but not her file) came into full view.

"I'm working on some special effects," she told Mrs. Wing. "For the home page. The only trouble is that it looks a little flashy."

"I like it," Mrs. Wing said when she saw the name Far Hills Junior High flashing in blue and red. "It's different."

"You do?" Madison asked. It had been almost a week since anyone had liked *anything* she did.

Mrs. Wing nodded enthusiastically. "I'm sure the other kids will like it, too."

"Waaaaaaaaaaaaaah!"

Madison looked into the stroller to see two small, pink hands poking up from the blankets. Phoebe wailed some more.

"Waaaaaaaaaaaaaah!"

"She's probably hungry," Mrs. Wing said, taking out a bottle and lifting Phoebe from the stroller and into her lap. Mrs. Wing started to feed the baby, cooing in her ear at the same time. Madison watched in awe as Phoebe calmed down and started sucking on the bottle.

"Is it hard?" Madison asked.

"Is what hard?" Mrs. Wing asked.

"Being a mom," Madison said.

Mrs. Wing laughed. "Oh, it's tough, sometimes. But it's so rewarding, too. Someday you'll know what I mean."

Madison couldn't imagine that far into the future. Right now she could barely imagine how she was going to get through the next month without her orange laptop.

"Hey, Madison, are you in here?" someone yelled from the doorway. Madison knew who it was. He'd managed to find her there every afternoon that week.

Lance.

"Mrs. Wing?!" Lance shouted when he saw their teacher. "Cool! What are you doing here again?"

"I came to pick up a few papers from Mr. Franks and visit briefly with some other teachers," she said. "Lance, are you here to help with the school site?"

"Oh, yeah, sure," Lance said.

Madison cringed.

It definitely gets worse before it gets better.

162

Why couldn't it have been Hart making a guest appearance in the computer lab, instead of Lance? Of course, Madison couldn't say anything grouchy, to make Lance leave. She didn't want to be rude in front of Mrs. Wing—and she couldn't be mean for no good reason.

Being nasty was how all of Madison's trouble had started!

"Well, I have to be taking off," Mrs. Wing said, putting Phoebe back into the stroller. She grabbed the pile of papers that had been left out for her and took a textbook off the shelf, too. Then she left a sealed envelope for Mr. Franks on the desk.

"I hope we'll see lots more of you," Madison said, wishing they were still alone in the lab. She could feel Lance's eyes on her.

"I hope that I'll come back for visits soon, too, Madison," Mrs. Wing said, reassuring her. "I want to keep up on all of your progress. And you, too, Lance!"

Lance giggled. "See you later, Mrs. Wing."

Mrs. Wing, with Phoebe, went out the door, jangling. Madison guessed it was Mrs. Wing's silver bangles that were making all the noise. It was like music to her ears—she missed her regular computer teacher that much.

Madison leaned down and grabbed her bag. "I'm outta here, too," she declared, zipping it up.

"But I just got here," Lance said.

"So?" Madison said. "See you in class tomorrow."

Before he could stop her, Madison dashed out of the lab and raced to her locker.

On the way down the hall, Madison spotted someone standing right in front of her locker door.

Ivy.

Madison wasn't surprised.

"I'm never going to forget, you know," Ivy growled.

Madison shrugged. "Elephants never forget," she said.

"Who are you calling . . ." Ivy looked shocked.

Madison eyed Ivy up and down. Her red hair didn't look quite as fluffy and perfect as usual. Nothing about Ivy looked perfect today. She looked *ugly*, Madison decided. Beauty was only skin deep, and all of Ivy's badness was showing through.

"*Oooooh!* You think you're *sooooo* smart, don't you?" Ivy said.

Madison looked at the notebook in Ivy's hands. She couldn't believe what she saw. On the front, doodled all over the notebook cover, were smiley faces.

Smiley faces!

Those were the exact same kind of smiley face that Madison had seen online on The Wall. If Ivy hadn't already, unknowingly, confessed to her mean acts, Madison would have considered those smiles major proof of Ivy's guilt.

Now Madison put on her own smiley face.

"I have to go," Madison snapped, closing her locker and slinging the orange bag over one shoulder.

"I know it was you, Maddie," Ivy said. "I know you wrote those lies about me. You're going to pay for that. You're going to pay."

Madison wanted to yell out, *Oh, yeah? Well, what kind of lies did you write about me? Who should really be the one paying!?*

But instead, she kept smiling and kept walking.

Madison remembered what Dad had said.

The way to win with Ivy Daly is NOT playing her game or by her rules. Fighting back gets you nowhere with some people, Maddie.

So Madison said nothing.

To her surprise, the silent treatment worked better against her enemy than anything else she'd ever tried. Madison always thought being speechless was a sign of weakness. But now it was a sign of power.

Poison Ivy didn't know what hit her. She couldn't fight against an opponent who didn't try to fight back.

And so Madison silently turned away from the enemy and walked down the hall, through the school doors, on to the sidewalk, and all the way home, without looking back once.

"Can I check my e-mail now, Mom?" Madison called out.

Mom was on a business call. She came out of her

office and placed the laptop on the kitchen table. Madison plugged it in silence.

She booted up the computer and went onto bigfishbowl.com.

Two messages were waiting.

FROM	SUBJECT
✉ BalletGrl	Can U Say Puppy?
✉ Bigwheels	I'm in TROUBLE

She clicked onto Aimee's message first.

```
From: BalletGrl
To: MadFinn, Wetwinz
Subject: Can U Say Puppy?
Date: Wed 15 Nov 3:11 PM
```
Today was the really big day!
We brought Blossom over to the clinic because she wasn't eating as much as usual and it turns out that it was just her insides. She's having puppies--can u believe it? It worked, FINALLY! After all the times trying. Hoorah!!

So, who wants the first puppy?

xoxoxox Aim

Madison was glad for Aimee and the other

Gillespies. New puppies would be coming in the new year. Madison couldn't wait to see them being born. She'd seen stuff like that only on the Discovery Channel. She wondered if Dan had been at the clinic when they had brought Blossom in.

After Aimee's message, Madison saw the second message from her keypal. She was super curious about the subject line and clicked on it.

From: Bigwheels
To: MadFinn
Subject: I'm in TROUBLE
Date: Wed 15 Nov 3:47 PM
___

Ready 4 this? I am grounded. Yeah--
ME! Have u ever been grounded? You
don't want to be. I can't leave my
room all week except 4 school. And
I'm breaking the rules by writing
this e-mail 2 u right now. Okay so
here's what happened. @ my sister's
b-day party the other day, I was
with this group of little kids and
I told them a scary story. I don't
know why I scared them--I just
felt like it. They were being so
annoying and it seemed funny at
the time. Well one of the mothers
complained to my mom that I was a
bad example and my mom TOTALLY
overreacted. So now I'm stuck. And

the worst part is that my little
sister is gloating about how she's
so sweet and I'm the "bad" one.
Could things get any worse?

**Madison laughed to herself when she read that.
She wanted to tell Bigwheels what she'd learned
only days before, about how things sometimes did
get worse—but about how they got better, too.
She kept reading.**

N e way, sorry 2 be so depresso,
but I hate being stuck inside. And
the week after I had all those
tests, too! It's not that warm out,
but I would rather be outside after
school. I guess I could go online
or something, but I'm bored w/The
Wall. It was funny @ first but I
dunno, now it seems dumb. How r u
doing?

I was thinking maybe we should
start our own bulletin board online
for keypals like us. We could call
it Keypal Palace or something like
that. Every room in the palace
would be like a different chat
room. A girl in my class @ school
told me she has a keypal like you.

168

Her keypal is in Europe. How cool
is that?

Well, write back soon. Until then,
I remain a prisoner! LOL.

Yours till the trouble makers,

Bigwheels, aka Vicki

Madison hit REPLY.

She couldn't wait to tell Bigwheels about her
own troublemaking week. She didn't want to brag
or anything; getting into the trouble she'd gotten
into wasn't much to brag about. In fact, it was just
plain embarrassing.

But maybe Bigwheels would find it comforting to
know that she wasn't the only one whose mom had
turned into a prison warden overnight.

Madison realized that she had spent a lot of time
over the past weeks worrying about being out of the
loop. But maybe she wasn't really so far out of it
after all.

She had her own loop right in front of her:
Aimee, Fiona, Lindsay, and, of course, Bigwheels.

With friends like those, it didn't matter so much
when things got a little off the wall. That special cir-
cle of friends would be there through everything—
online and off.

Mad Chat Words:

```
8>O            Uh-oh!
>=]            Sneaky grin
WAY?           What about you?
GOOH           Get out of here!
m8             Mate
CML            Call me later
NY             Not yet
<GRRR>         I'm soooo angry
O&O            Over and out
GOIA           Get over it already
*G*            Giggle
1daful         Wonderful
```

Madison's Computer Tip

After my experience on The Wall, I've sworn off online bulletin boards. Boy, did I learn my lesson. **Beware of online gossip.** It can be anonymous—and dangerous. Plus, you never know who's posting with a fake screen name. Before you know it, you could even be the next target. I don't regret the fact that Ivy got a taste of her own medicine, but I do regret *how* it happened. I'm going to be a lot more careful when surfing on sites like The Wall in the future. And I won't ever post nasty messages about anyone else—ever.

Visit Madison at www.madisonfinn.com